TERROR IN BIG BEND

ETHAN RICHARDS

SEVEREDPRESS

TERROR IN BIG BEND

WWW.SEVEREDPRESS.COM

ISBN: 978-1-923165-20-5

PROLOGUE

Big Bend State Park
Presidio County, Texas

The brutal Texas sun beat down on the brandy-tinted sands of Big Bend State Park. Big Bend—the great geological crossroads of the Appalachian Mountains, the Rockies, and the Trans-Pecos Volcanic Field. The Bofecillos Mountains reached skyward, their peaks penetrating the blue sky. The rugged beauty of their rock faces dwarfed even the works of Michelangelo or da Vinci. Sparse vegetation painted the Chihuahuan Desert in a piebald coat of beige and green.

Heat waves, visible to the human eye, shimmered skyward from the sandy soil. Years past, a cement mixer from a construction truck had been altered and painted to look like a NASA space capsule. It had served as a tourist destination, bringing thousands of visitors to this specific spot—the Cerro de las Burras Loop.

Enrique Esparza had parked his four-wheeled, all-terrain vehicle on the Cerro de las Burras Loop inside the park before he ran six miles along the rocky trail. Solar rays beat down on the trail, heating the soil below Enrique. The pain of a long, arduous run combined with the intense West Texas sun sapped his strength and energy. Enrique winced as the stitch in his side grew harder. He wore nothing except for his wristwatch, cross-country shoes, and blue running shorts with the Presidio Blue Devils Cross Country logo.

In an agonizing gait, Enrique shambled toward that mock spacecraft. He winced as salt from his heavy perspiration crept past his eyelids and stung his eyes. His olive-colored skin glowed from the sweat as he peered at his wristwatch.

"I'll get them next time." He angrily shook his head. "I'll run fast—"

Enrique gritted his teeth and kicked at a pile of sand-colored rocks. He yelled, slamming a fist against his quad.

"Ten seconds off!" he howled. "Ten seconds off!"

He paced in circles, placing his hands on his hips and attempting to catch his breath. There are two types of runners: athletes and competitors. Enrique was the latter, pushing his body to the limit. While Enrique had heart, it hadn't been noticed by the college scouts. Now, his only option was to walk on to a collegiate cross-country program. Enrique's father had earned a scholarship while running cross-country at

1

West Texas A&M University. He wanted to be a good son. He wanted to follow in his father's footsteps and reduce the financial burden on his family.

"Yeah, Enrique," he said. "Who needs a scholarship?"

But he knew he did. His mother had picked up a part-time job to pay for his senior ring. His mother, proud to help, had already applied for full-time employment around Presidio County.

I'm making my mom work. I dishonor mi familia!

Enrique reached down, picked up a rock, and hurled it in frustration.

BANG!

The rock bounced off the truck cement mixer.

He continued to pace.

Meow.

Enrique's stomach twisted. Had he just hurt an animal? With his remaining energy, he bounded to the cement mixer and looked inside.

Un gato, he thought, staring at the orange tabby inside the enigmatic vessel. From his time in Presidio High School science classes, he learned that feral cats howled with eerie human-like shrieks. Still, it was domesticated cats that "meowed."

Meow.

"You're lucky, Mr. Gato," he said. "I was just two steps away from hopping on my four-wheeler and driving out of here."

Enrique shook his head. "You cats do weird things, but *why* did you go in there?"

The cat, still inside the mixer, walked toward Enrique. It crept across and sniffed Enrique's hand.

"*Pero*," Enrique said. "I don't know why cats do anything."

He pressed his head into the opening of the mock spacecraft and reached his arm inside, offering the cat an escape.

"Ps-ps-ps-ps," he said. "Let me help you, *gato.*"

The cat hissed. It arched its back.

"Que?" Enrique yanked his hand back.

He stepped back, rubbing the hand that had been inside. As he did, a chill crept up his spine. He spun around, his knees quivering and hands trembling.

"Hello?" He looked around. *"¿Quién es?"*

With nervous movement, Enrique shuffled left to right, scanning the immediate area of the Cerro de las Burras Loop.

Then, he saw it.

Que tipo de animal is that? Enrique thought, but in reality, he knew the answer. Presidio International School had earned national recognition for its educational system, with its science and mathematics programs in particular. Teachers from around the world, wishing to earn a work visa in the United States, would be sent to Presidio. As a result, some of the best educators on the planet could be found here. His AP Paleontology teacher, Mr. Agila, had taught him well. Despite the impossibility of the situation, Enrique recognized what the monster was.

"Pero, yo sé lo que es." Enrique whispered, *"Sé lo que es."*

Despite its massive size, the monster seemed to emerge from its surroundings. Its tawny-colored flesh matched the color of the desert Presidio County soil.

The creature stood on four thick limbs, looming seven feet tall. Its snout was covered in proto-mammalian whiskers that looked like quills. Wispy hairs sparsely decorated the beast's rough walrus-like epidermis that stretched over its thirty-foot-long frame. Its terrible eyes were mustard-tinted orbs with black vertical slits.

"Porque es a Gorgonopsian synapsid *aqui?"* Enrique said aloud.

How did that sneak up on me? Enrique trembled like an addict savaged by a chemical withdrawal. The beast didn't move in a straightforward motion but at angles similar to the movements of a puma, reminding Enrique of a jujitsuka reaching in at an opponent.

Somehow, the primordial beast had been resurrected and now roamed Big Bend State Park.

Enrique needed to get on his ATV. He needed to get out of Big Bend. He knelt, picking up another rock. If he could hit the field, it might distract the monster long enough for Enrique to jump onto his four-wheeler and drive off.

Despite his fear, life-threatening danger and confusion gripped him.

Como es possible?

Enrique hurled the rock.

It bounced off the rough skin. Enrique sprinted toward his four-wheeler.

The abominable thing launched forward.

In a feline-like motion, it raised its right paw.

WHAAM!

The gargantuan paw struck Enrique's chest. He flew backward and slammed into the ground. Mesquite leaves and other painful pieces of Texas plant life lacerated his flesh. Jumping to his feet, Enrique crept sideways, next to the abandoned cement mixer.

He looked around the area, searching for the creature.

It was gone.

Suddenly, a force slammed into Enrique's back. He screamed in pain, his voice a foul falsetto as fangs penetrated his right shoulder.

Adrenaline pumped through his body. Despite the bloodletting, he charged forward, attempting to get to his ATV.

The Gorgon lunged. Horrible fangs latched onto Enrique's right leg. The Gorgonopsian synapsid shook its head, left to right. The serrated teeth dug deeper with each motion.

"*Ayúdame!*" Enrique cried, hoping some passerby might hear him. "*Ayúdame!*"

His pleas only echoed through the canyons and mountains.

Despite the overwhelming pain, Enrique was still a fighter. With surprising strength, the Presidio Blue Devil pounded his fists against the primordial animal's elongated skull. He threw his right fist into its eye. The terrestrial demon howled.

Enrique, feeling a slight release in pressure, struck again.

The Gorgon cried again, then slung his head leftward.

Enrique flew through the air.

BAAM!

Enrique's leg slammed straight into the square hole of the cement mixer. The metal cut into his leg, penetrating his muscles and locking him in place. He tumbled over, but the heavy bruising made his movements slow. His broken leg was now trapped inside the cement mixer's window.

Enrique hung upside down. In his weak state, his arms hung out in an inverted "v." His now-disfigured leg trapped him helplessly against the modified cement mixer.

"*Ayúdame!*" he cried, but his voice failed, managing only a hoarse whisper.

He could see the entirety of the monster.

The great Gorgonopsian Synapsid. It looked like a lean, terrestrial walrus.

"Why are you here?" Enrique asked.

Soft steps carried the beast forward. The thing pressed its snout skyward as if trying to understand the situation. As it did, Enrique saw that his killer's right eye was swollen shut.

"At least I didn't go down without a fight," he whispered, his voice a decrescendo with the continued blood loss. The Gorgonopsian growled as if answering Enrique's challenge. It pulled back its lips, revealing its scarlet-stained fangs.

Enrique shuddered as he watched his own blood dripping into the monster's mouth.

"*En Tus manos encomiendo mi espíritu,*" he whispered.

The creature leapt forward, mouth agape, baring its terrible fangs.

Enrique had lost too much blood to scream.

In his last few seconds of mortality, he watched as the Gorgonopsian devoured his bowels.

TERROR IN BIG BEND

PART I

"Big Bend allows no winners; there are only survivors." ---Kenneth Baxter Ragsdale

CHAPTER 1

Jorge Mondragon

Texas State Park Police Officer Jorge Mondragon watched as men in white hazmat suits worked to remove the remains of Enrique Esparaza. Enrique's body hung upside down from the decorated cement mixer, making his removal a difficult challenge.

"It's been a while since something like this happened on this side of the border," Texas State Trooper Joseph Manning said.

Jorge balled his hands into fists, his knuckles white, as he thought of the implications of a potential border war. He turned his head and spat as his whole body burned with anger. Before graduating from the Texas Game Warden Academy, Jorge had done twenty years with the Texas Army National Guard, most of his time in the 1st Battalion, 143 Airborne Infantry Regiment. Between state-side disasters and combat deployments, Jorge had witnessed ghastly scenes.

But this macabre imagery dwarfed the past.

Enrique had been pinned against the cement mixer and then ripped open. The left leg fell into the mixer as they tore at his corpse, attempting to free it.

"We got something else back here," one of the workers called out.

Something smacked the interior wall of the cement mixer.

Jorge's hands gripped the pistol grip of his Glock.

"No worries!" the man closest to the cement mixer said, looking inside. *"Solamente un gato!"*

"How the heck did a cat get in there?" the Texas State Trooper called.

"I gotta see this," Jorge said, walking toward the gore-stained square opening. He looked in.

A big furry ball hit him in the chest. Involuntarily, he caught the cat in his arms.

"Hey there, grouch-o." Joseph Manning patted Jorge on the back. "He seems to like you."

The cat purred and pressed its head against Jorge's chest.

"I'm not a cat-person," Jorge rolled his eyes.

"Heck, Jorge," Manning teased. "You ain't much of a people-person either."

After graduating from the Texas State Game Warden Academy in Hamilton, Jorge had chosen to work in Big Bend. He'd picked the location, not just because of the desert's beauty but because the area's vastness allowed him to avoid people.

"This cat has to be put down." Jorge's face twisted in disgust.

"Ah, just because he invaded your personal space?" Manning laughed.

"No!" Jorge held up the cat, allowing Manning to see. "Look."

Bits of gore clung to the cat's whiskers. While in the National Guard, Jorge had been sent on domestic missions, including hurricane relief. During those missions, he learned that if a domestic animal ate a person, it had to be put down.

"You don't know that the cat actually... *ate* Enrique," Manning stopped himself, his face turning off-color. "That's the only thing I've ever seen that you got along with, Jorge."

The cat continued to purr and rub its head against Jorge. Jorge lifted one hand and stroked the cat's head.

"See, that thing is good for you," Manning said.

Jorge yanked his hand away as if burnt, then, taking the cat, he put it into the vehicle. He turned on the truck, allowing the air conditioning to keep the cat safe.

"You still don't know if that cat did what you think it did," Manning said.

"Can't take the risk. I don't want that thing running around in my park."

Manning lifted his eyebrows. "Dead cats are nothing compared to what we might be seeing."

Jorge sighed. "I can agree with you there."

CHAPTER 2

Jorge Mondragon

The cat stayed in Jorge's vehicle until his portion of the investigation was complete. Despite the need for the cat's destruction, he had allowed the animal into his truck with the air conditioning running.

Jorge opened his truck door and got in.

THUMP! He slammed the door behind.

"Whoa!" Jorge yelled as the muck-caked cat jumped into his lap. His eyes bulged as he studied the feline as it purred with motor-like fury.

"Most people give me a lotta space," Jorge said.

As if to say, *"But I'm not most people,"* the cat's purring grew louder. It rubbed its body against Jorge's chest, leaving long strands of fur pinned to his vest.

Jorge sighed. And with slow, hesitant hands, he petted the cat.

"What a day, Mr. Gato," Jorge said.

He stared out the window. It wasn't just Enrique's horrific death. No, it was fatigue. Jorge was tired.

"I'm too young to feel this old," he said. His knees cracked as he stretched his legs. As he moved, the cat's tail snapped left to right. Jorge put his hands on the cat to push him to the side.

The cat playfully bit Jorge.

"Don't get too comfortable," he said, glancing at the cat in his passenger seat. "Tomorrow, you still got the Big Adios."

The cat disregarded the information, instead purring and rolling in circles.

"Is there something about me," Jorge said, "that you can see, but no one else can? I ain't exactly cuddly."

Jorge couldn't take the cat to the veterinarian's office until the morning.

"Let's go home, Mr. Gato," Jorge said and threw his vehicle into drive.

***

"Mr. Gato," Jorge grabbed the cat, opened his unit door, and began walking toward his house. "I am so tired that I am willing to let a flesh-eating punk like you stay in my house."

Holding the cat in his left hand, he walked up to the residence the park provided, opened the door, and entered.

"You're lucky there, Mr. Gato," Jorge carried the cat toward his laundry room. "If you'd met me previously, you woulda been staying the night in a houseboat on the docks of Lake Phantom."

He dropped his arm. The cat leapt forward, purring as it did.

"Great," Jorge grunted. He glanced at the cat. He wasn't a zoologist, so he couldn't describe a cat's emotions, but as the cat rolled in circles, he feared it to be a display of gratitude.

He gritted his teeth. Mr. Gato *had* to be put down.

Looking at the animal only reminded Jorge of what happened at the park. "Enrique was a good kid," he said aloud. "One of the best of them."

But Jorge's respect of Enrique and love of his town had been lost on everyone. Jorge had watched Enrique's cross-country meets. He had seen the tenacity with which the teenager sprinted across the finish line, passing out from the maximum effort. But Jorge wasn't much of a smiler. He might have been visible in the community, but as he himself said, he wasn't exactly "cuddly." Most of the town had been slightly intimidated by the strange new lawman who had moved to the area.

"Enrique's style wasn't a runner," Jorge whispered. "He was a competitor—a fighter."

Natural athletes could run, regardless of external factors, but not Enrique. Enrique liked to compete. In terms of running, he was a head-hunter, chasing down his rivals and putting his body in pain as he increased his speed to pass.

"*Pero* if what I think will happen does occur," Jorge said to himself, "he won't be the only good kid we lose."

Jorge Mondragon shuddered at the implications. Criminal organizations in Central America were more potent than most state actors. Military leaders and political think-tanks had debated the benefits of war with the growing threat.

War.

While the Great War ruined Europe, the Mexican Border War, or Bandit Wars, kept terror and war on North American soil. It lasted from 1910 to 1919, killing almost one thousand soldiers from the United States and Mexico.

That had been with turn-of-the-century technology, he thought. *How many more soldiers would die in a border war now?*

Of course, Enrique deserved justice, but the conflict could cost even more lives. Jorge looked down at the black bracelet that encircled his wrist. His whole body started to shake.

"You know what?" he said aloud. "I think I got an answer for this."

Closing his eyes, he breathed deep—controlling his breath, counting in for four seconds, holding it for the same time, and releasing it. Feeling his body returning to normal, he stood up and returned to the laundry room.

"I can feel bad about your destruction tomorrow." He hoisted the cat up from the confined space's floor. He should have called animal control. But the blood-soaked images had distracted him from following procedures.

"But tonight, Mr. Gato," Jorge said, "I want a friend."

CHAPTER 3

Jorge Mondragon

Jorge woke to the violent hiss of the cat. The jeering cat leapt on Jorge's bed, running across his chest before bouncing off and into the closet.

"*No se* if that's loyalty," he said, feeling his chest. "*Pero* I guess it's a warning."

Jorge winced at the minor cuts from the cat's claws. His years of tactical training taught him when and where to ignore details and how to not overthink things, but an animal reacting weirdly was always a strong hint of bad juju.

Pero why ain't Rehoboam going crazy? he thought.

Wild donkeys lived in the Big Bend area. Jorge caught one and kept it on his property as early detection. The beast's braying served him better than any security system and required less maintenance.

But now, Rehoboam remained silent.

Jorge jumped up from his bed. He threw on clothes and boots, grabbed his Glock and flashlight, and in an excellent sur position, made his way to his front door.

In the past, migrants avoiding legal entrance had come through this area, and a few times, they had come to his house, seeking water.

The terrain was tough, and it bred tough people. Tough people could be good or bad, but personal safety was paramount in an isolated area like this. He peered through the shades, trying to reduce his signature as much as possible. Then, seeing no immediate threat, Jorge opened the door and walked outside. He stepped into the night, under the violet star-studded sky.

While his spine tingled, his rational brain couldn't quite see the problem. But despite the lack of evidence, Jorge could tell—no, *feel*—that something was different.

He scanned the area. His eyes first went skyward, looking for anomalies. Finally, his gaze fell to the ground. He studied the sand and sediments underneath his feet.

"There," he said. "That's what's different."

Jorge scratched his head as he studied the sign. The soil looked like waves in the ocean. Sand arched up; little rocks pressed to the side of the flattened area. It was as if someone had hauled a barrel across the ground or had tried to iron down the sand, but as a result, sediment went on either side.

But stranger still was the lack of sign from Rehoboam. He had come to Rehoboam's corner, where he usually found the ass. He started a clover-leaf pattern from the waves of sand, looking for any evidence of Rehoboam.

"Bingo," he said as he lowered the flashlight more parallel to the ground. By tilting it, he could see the differences in the angle of sand that created the print. He saw the circular sign and the pressed-up sand that made a halo around it.

"That looks like a donkey snow angel," he laughed. Just above Rehoboam's prints was the imprint of the creature's profile.

"So," Jorge turned his flashlight to the waves, "something smashed against the ground. Rehoboam was right here." He illuminated the hoofmarks before turning to the "snow angel."

"And then right here, Rehoboam just vanishes."

For the next hour, Jorge went in circles around his property, and despite the time of night, he called out for his beast. To the untrained eye, Jorge was looking at dirt. But when it came to sign-cutting, Jorge Mondragon was a Texan Sherlock Holmes. Forensic scientists trained at Scotland Yard would have stood in awe at his investigative abilities. He edged his flashlight, manipulating its illuminating properties.

He angled his head toward the ground. The bits of dirt now seemed like great mountains, with each divot transforming into spurs and draws all telling a different story. But despite this—despite his expertise:

Jorge Mondragon found nothing.

The ground seemed as if it had been flattened. As if a giant sheet had smashed against the dirt, clearing any sign. Smugglers and migrants were known to walk with carpeted shoes or tie bovine hooves to their boots. But when a sign was covered—more sign was created. He searched the flattened earth to no avail.

Rehoboam was gone.

Jorge scratched his head, turned off his flashlight, and returned to his house. Rehoboam hadn't been a small creature. He had been about fifteen hands tall, with thick equine muscles.

"Donkey rustling?" he shook his head.

Cattle and horse rustling happened in these parts, but Rehoboam had been a feral burro. The great beast had been one of the Big Bend wild donkeys before Jorge had caught and broken him. There were programs that allowed people to catch and own these creatures.

"Why rustle mine?" he asked aloud as he entered his house. "How did a thousand-pound animal just disappear?"

CHAPTER 4

The Gorgon

The creature—the great Gorgonopsian replicant—licked its dagger-like fangs, savoring this strange new taste. The aroma was so strong he could taste it.

Human words and emotions couldn't describe the taste. The monster was warm. It could feel the taste of blood over its whole body. It had tasted human flesh before—but never like this. Before, it hadn't been a challenge. He had consumed the souls—bound and gagged.

But Enrique was different.

Enrique had been a fighter. The blood of the Tarahumara had coursed through his veins! The Tarahumara—the great warriors who never submitted to their Conquistador oppressors, instead fighting and making their home in the harsh Chihuahuan Desert.

But Enrique's family hadn't stayed in Mexico. They had gone north to gain citizenship in the Great American Republic. They found a new adopted Motherland—the United States—the Nation that won World War II and defeated the Axis Powers. That great Nation that defeated Russia in the Space Race by victoriously burying its banner on the surface of the moon.

The fighting spirit of his culture had grown even stronger when they became Texans. A tenacious combination—the ichor of the undefeated Tarahumara people with spirit cultivated by his Texan homeland.

And that spirit—that refusal to surrender—had only sweetened the kill!

Most man-eaters, like tigers, lions, and sharks, make a kill by either mistaking their target or prey switching.

But while others found human flesh unnatural, it created a new desire for the creature. Its mind, its whole body, hummed with excitement.

It wasn't simply hunger:

It was lust.

CHAPTER 5

Jorge Mondragon

Jorge slowed down as he approached the herd of bovine creatures crowding FM 170 East near the Upper and Lower Madera. He had his windows barely cracked. His tactical background had taught him to roll them down slightly, but not all the way, enabling him to both hear and smell.

"This is strange," Jorge said. While cattle did walk along FM 170, they typically didn't travel up these more complex areas. Jorge winced. Should he leave his vehicle to scout the best path or continue driving forward?

Here goes nothing. He began weaving his truck through the organic obstacles clogging the road.

"Help!" a voice cried out.

Jorge scanned the area. He spotted a tall man with a shock of red hair and a graying goatee. Jorge flashed his overhead lights, letting the man know he saw him.

"It just scooped him," the man said, pointing up the steep mountain beside them, "then yanked him up that."

The man gesticulated in an insane manner and pointed toward the sky.

Jorge parked his truck, pulled out his keys, and walked toward the man. "What's going on—"

A cow mooed.

"My name is Brody Jennison," the man said, then continued pointing upward. "My friend—he got scooped up."

"Who did what?"

Brody shook his head, "No, no 'who,' but 'what'."

Jorge leaned forward, sniffing the air.

"It's a vape," Brody held up his item. "I'm not high."

"What are you trying to say?"

"I'm saying it wasn't a person." Brody shaded his eyes with his hand. "An animal—it came from the mountain, grabbed my friend, and ran back up."

"Up that?" Jorge pointed to the near vertical cliff face of the canyon.

"Yes!" Brody yelled. "Some kind of animal!"

An animal? Jorge thought. While any creature's ascent up that cliff was impossible, he couldn't help but think about Enrique's body. Cartels did demonstrate that level of violence, but an actual creature, in this particular case, might make more sense.

"Let's go find him!" Brody said. "I saw the creature. Take me through the park."

"Whoa," Jorge raised his hands. His stomach twisted as the man pled for access to his truck.

"My friend," Brody said.

"Was it a bear?"

Brody snorted. "No."

"Mountain lion?"

"Something like that."

"What does that mean?"

"It means, just like I said. Kinda... weird... an unknown thing... but still... kinda familiar."

Cattle continued to cry out.

"What do you mean?" Jorge asked.

"Like..." Brody pinched at his skin. "Like... in your subconscious..."

Jorge leaned forward and sniffed the air. Painful tears filled his eyes as a familiar skunk-like odor stung his nostrils.

"Are you high?" Jorge asked.

"What?" Brody yelled. "No... I mean... that's not the point."

Jorge sighed and shook his head. "Turn around and place your hands in the small of your back."

Brody sighed and turned around. Jorge grabbed his handcuffs and started walking forward.

Suddenly, Brody ran. Dust shot skyward as his feet beat against the ground in a frantic rhythm.

"No se mueva!" Jorge shouted and sprinted after Brody.

Jorge leaped through the air—a beautiful form tackle—slamming Brody into the ground. Brody's head bounced off the gravel-covered desert soil. Specks of blood shot into the air. Jorge continued pushing Brody down and yanked one hand back, pinning it into the small of his back.

Brody—despite Jorge's strength—yanked his hand free.

"Wait!" Brody cried out. "Wait!"

Jorge wrapped a handcuff around Brody's pinned wrist.

"Look!" Brody cried. "Just give me a second—"

Jorge yanked the other hand back.

"Stop!" Brody screamed.

"Just calm down," Jorge whispered.

"There!" Brody spat and a glob of saliva splattered onto the ground. "Look at that!"

Jorge winced, expecting to be hit. He pulled back and his hand went limp. He released his grip and stood up.

"What are you doing?" Brody yelled. Then, his voice grew softer. "What are you doing?"

Jorge stepped away from Brody and took a knee next to the spit. Taking his flashlight from his duty belt, he angled it in a perpendicular manner.

The light hit the ground, making the miniscule particles of sand appear as mountains.

"It doesn't make any sense," Jorge muttered.

Brody squirmed on his stomach, "Now, do you believe me?"

Jorge kept his eyes on the ground.

"You gonna pull a Derek Chauvin and let me die in handcuffs?" Brody spat.

"For my safety and for yours," Jorge sighed, "I should keep you in those things, but…"

Jorge studied the ground. A giant footprint scarred the dirt. The heel strike was rounded, almost feline, but five claws, similar to a bear, pressed against the sand. But while the strange print had similarities to a bear, it dwarfed even a polar bear print.

"You saw this thing?" Jorge pointed at the sign.

Brody nodded.

"Well," Jorge said, staring at the print. "Let's go find your *amigo*."

CHAPTER 6

The Gorgon

The Gorgon carried Brody's friend, Tennyson Johnston, in his gore-stained mouth. Deeper the monster trod into the Chihuahuan Desert, with Tennyson's limp body. Its great saber teeth pinned the Californian in place.

Tennyson wasn't dead—not yet. The monster's thick, primeval saliva penetrated Tennyson's wounds, keeping the man from dying.

The monster couldn't explain it, but this man with THC-filled veins tasted different. The creature's senses didn't change, but he noticed all associated sensations. He didn't simply taste this man's blood; the smell of iron erupted in his nasal cavities. Other chemicals, adrenaline and those associated with shock, added flavor to the half-dead man.

"Just... kill me," Tennyson Johnston whispered from lacerated lips.

The Gorgon's eyes lit with zeal at the stoned man's squeals. This eldritch creation, the synapsid replicant, had been given curious tastes. He had learned he preferred human flesh, but not those fed to him, as it had been in the past. No, he liked to hunt. He wanted his prey to be alive.

And this man not only had to try to flee but was seasoned with the strange narcotic. The land leviathan's whole body shook with excitement. He had gorged himself and couldn't eat the man now, but his savory skin was too great to let escape. The Gorgon could store him, let the man try to escape, and sharpen his skills in a manner identical to a cat or an orca. Saliva dripped from his mouth as he grew in excitement. The half-dead man coughed as a slimy mass dripped over his face.

The Gorgon looked skyward, searching for his trail. Then, with Tennyson still in its grasp, it made its trek toward El Solitario—the volcano overlooking Big Bend.

CHAPTER 7

Jorge Mondragon

"First, I saved a stupid cat," Jorge shook his head and looked over at Brody, who sat in the passenger seat of his police unit. "I must be turning into some sort of bleedin' heart."

Brody tilted his head at Jorge, inspecting the law enforcement officer. "I really doubt that, warden."

"It's Officer," Jorge pointed at his badge.

"Well, if we're going to get technical," Brody dusted off imaginary dust from his shoulder, "I'm a doctor of veterinary medicine."

Jorge laughed. He felt his stomach muscles press against the armored vest under his shirt.

"*No se mamas!*" Jorge snorted.

"Before this life was thrust on me," Brody's voice grew softer, and he looked through the passenger side window.

"No, you weren't," Jorge shook his head. "As a law enforcement officer, I'm trained to listen to my gut and my gut says that makes no sense."

"Hmm." Brody scratched his chin. "It's good you listen to your gut. But that commonsense approach has its flaws. If you think that way, you're limited only to experience."

"Ah, you just listened to your mind?" Jorge chortled. "You don't think Miss Mary Jane has hurt that a little?"

"I'm not completely gone," Brody shook his head.

"Sammy Davis Jr. was right," Jorge said.

"Sammy Davis Jr?" Brody asked. "Now you're not making any sense, Officer."

"I mainly listen to bluegrass and *norteño*. But that song, Mr. Bojangles," Jorge smiled. "It's about a man in jail talking about life... the big picture. It's about the philosophical conversations that occur after someone gets thrown in jail."

"But I'm not in jail," Brody said.

"Only because I need your mind. *Pero,* tell me, what were you about to say?"

"The medical world treated my back injury. They gave me pain meds. Unlike you, I didn't rely on experience, I relied on science. Those who I trusted recommended strong medications, and..."

"You got addicted?" Jorge said.

Brody nodded. "Marijuana released me from my addiction."

"Muy intersante."

"No." Brody continued to look outside. "Sad. I didn't want this lifestyle. Not for me. And especially not for my..."

Jorge's stomach grew weak as the conversation grew heavier.

You should be sign-cutting, Jorge thought. He had avoided people for so long. While in the military, Jorge had been around soldiers for an intense amount of time. He had shared foxholes and used public showers. When Jorge retired, he had made it a goal to be left alone. And there, for a time, he had convinced himself that it was good.

Attempting to remain subtle, Jorge looked at Brody out the corner of his eye.

The reality is he missed a good conversation, and this alleged former doctor of veterinary science and present deadhead provided that. He grabbed the flashlight from his belt and rolled down his window. He turned the device on and angled it at the ground.

"What are you doing?" Brody yelled.

"Looking for prints—"

"You can't do that! I've seen that thing. It'll rip you out of the car." Brody grabbed him by the arm.

This is what I get for trusting people, he thought.

"Calma se la berga!" Jorge shouted.

"Close the window!" Brody yelled and continued to pull on Jorge's arm.

Jorge slammed his foot against the brake. He threw the truck in park. He undid his seat belt, but it didn't wholly slide off him because he moved so fast. The loose belt still hung across his vest, just under his chin.

Jorge pushed against Brody's chest with both hands, pinning him against the truck wall.

"I didn't want to put you in cuffs," Jorge started.

"The window! Why did you roll it down..."

Brody's voice grew into incoherent screams as he waved his hands in an erratic fashion.

And despite this chaos, despite Brody's unhinged movement and screams, Jorge heard something:

The heavy footfall against the rugged Texas terrain.

Something was approaching.

With Brody still pinned, Jorge turned to see the oncoming noise. The seat belt scratched his chin as he looked outside.

The footfalls grew louder.

WHAAM!

A massive, unstoppable force slammed into the police truck. The truck rose, balancing on the passenger side tires. For what felt like an eternity, the car stood on end. The seat belt scratched Jorge's chin.

WHAAM!

Something struck the truck a second time. This time, there was no balancing. The great Park Police vehicle slammed onto its side before falling over. It landed with its roof on the ground.

In the chaotic cycle, the seat belt wrapped around Jorge's throat. The weight of his body slammed into the seat belt. It dug further into his throat, silencing him.

"Ayúdame," he tried to say in a horrible, constricted whisper.

But it was too late. The oxygen was running from his body. Technicolor tints burst into his half-closed eyes.

With fading cognizance, Jorge pawed at his vest, feeling for his knife.

If I could just cut the belt.

But as he moved, the belt grew tighter. The whole world went dark.

Jorge's eyes slammed shut.

PART II

"The desert will scour your soul." - Edward Abbey

CHAPTER 8

Jorge Mondragon

"Give him some space!" a voice called in a heavy Texas lowland accent.

Jorge's eyes peeled open. He lay on Big Bend State Park's hard desert floor. Several strangers leaned over him, staring at him in his vulnerable state.

Jorge rose in a coffin setup. He reached for his Glock only to find his holster empty.

"Hola!" a voice called out. *"Estas con amigos."*

Jorge's eyes bulged as he looked around.

Four men were standing around him.

"We're friends," said a bald-headed Hispanic man with a handlebar mustache painted with thick, paint-like gel. He wore a digital camouflage uniform with blue nitrile gloves.

"I know this park." Jorge touched his throat. He winced as his fingers ran over the lacerations on his throat. "But I don't know you."

"Fair 'nough." The man pulled off his blue nitrile gloves and stuck out his right hand to shake. "My name is Everrett Pacheco. My compadres dubbed me 'Mustache.'"

Jorge searched his gut, trying to find the correct response. With great hesitancy, he accepted Mustache's handshake.

"Fitting," Jorge said. "You're the one who saved me?"

"Nah," the man's voice rang thick with what Jorge guessed to be a Rio Grande Valley accent. "Your amigo over there. He pulled you out, kept you safe, and flagged us down."

"My..." Jorge adjusted his collar, *"amigo?"*

Jorge hadn't felt he'd made friends since he retired from the National Guard. Now, a stranger hadn't only befriended him but saved him too.

"Yeah, that feller over there." Mustache pointed at a tall, lanky white man with unkempt red hair and a soul patch under his bottom lip. The man wore blue jeans and boots, an over-sized tie-dyed shirt, and a peace sign.

"Brody?" Jorge's voice reached high into the treble clef. "He saved me?"

"You'd have been a goner," Mustache said. "You're lucky to have him around."

Jorge gave an awkward smile and nodded at Brody. Brody returned the acknowledgment.

"Here," Mustache handed Jorge a jug of water. He accepted it and got to his feet. He tilted his head back and drank. His throat stung, but he hydrated anyway.

Swallowing the water, Jorge looked around the group.

With the exception of Brody, everyone wore digital-style camouflage. Mustache had a long gun slung behind his back, but the others wore full tactical vests and slung shotguns.

"What are you guys doing out here?" Jorge asked. "You guys... hunters?"

"Hmmm," Mustache twirled the edge of his mustache, "I guess you could say that."

CHAPTER 9

Jorge Mondragon

"First things first," Mustache said, standing next to Jorge. "You gotta concussion."

Jorge ignored Mustache and scanned the area. He wasn't sure of their exact location, but he knew they were still in Big Bend State Park. A pinkish cloud painted the darkening sky, giving a faint illumination to the room. He was still determining where in the park he had been recovered.

"First things first?" Jorge squeaked and rubbed his throat. "I could have figured I'd been concussed, but that ain't the first question I got. Like, who are you guys? *De donde?* And *que* hit my truck?"

"All good questions," Mustache said.

"And yet still, you ain't answering," Jorge said, crossing his arms over his chest.

"You'll have to excuse my friend," Brody said, putting his hand on Jorge's shoulder. "His bedside manner is wanting."

"I'll say it is," Mustache muttered under his breath.

"That thing that hit your truck," Brody said. "That was a pair of bulls."

"Bulls?" Jorge continued to look around. "A pair? That doesn't make any sense."

"No," Brody laughed, "no sense at all. But that's what it was. That cattle got lost, and two huge bulls were running around as well. One knocked us halfway, and the other finished us off."

"And that's not going to make any sense," Mustache said. "Not until we talk a little bit more."

Jorge cast a skeptical glance at Mustache. "If this wasn't my territory—as in the State Park," he said, "I'd be a lot more friendly, but..."

"No, you wouldn't," a voice said.

Jorge turned to see a taller man with shoulder-length jet-colored hair knotted in a tight ponytail. On his tactical vest was a sewn silver badge with the initial BIA.

Jorge squinted, trying to read more about the man's uniform.

"Your name is Jorge Mondragon," the BIA agent said. "We tried reaching out to you but, unfortunately, this is how we ended up."

"Feds," Jorge muttered.

"My name is Felix American Pony. I'm with the Bureau of Indian Affairs," the man said.

"You've been roaming around this park without trying to network with local agencies?" Jorge balled his hands into fists.

"Hey, brother," Mustache interjected. "I'd call this situation... unprecedented."

"Feds overreaching their bounds?" Jorge chortled. "That ain't new."

Jorge's blood grew hot. When he'd served overseas in a conventional unit, units from the special operations community would conduct unilateral and unknown missions in their area of operations. The negative backlash would fall onto the landowners. History was now repeating itself, with a clandestine federal team patrolling his park. Ranches and farmlands were going to be destroyed and he was going to have to deal with the aftermath.

"You're right, Mondragon, Feds overstepping bounds isn't exactly new." Felix American Pony handed Jorge a screen-protected tablet-like device. "But, this is."

Jorge's blood felt like ice. He shivered as the feeling of hot anger was replaced with the coolness of shock. His stomach flipped and his mouth went dry.

The screen showed a picture of the footprint he had seen with Brody. The massive, eldritch horror imprinted on the sandy soil of Big Bend State Park.

CHAPTER 10

Jorge Mondragon

Jorge gulped, pointing at the tablet, "You know what this is?"

Felix American Pony nodded, "Yep."

"Well," Jorge tugged at his collar. "Can you tell me?"

"As you'd say in the military," Felix said, "you gotta set the conditions."

Jorge squinted, studying this tall figure that stood in front of him. Felix American Pony.

The man stood over six feet tall with solid aquiline features, pronounced cheekbones, and thin, dark, almost purple lips. His tactical setup showed a high level of professionalism.

"All these guys here are BIA?" Jorge asked. "If so, why does that guy have a Japanese flag on his uniform?"

"Again," Felix said, "let me set the conditions."

"Fine," Jorge put his hands on his hips. "Talk to me."

CHAPTER 11

Jorge Mondragon

"I got two questions," Mustache held up two fingers.

Jorge remained in the group's center in the Big Bend State Park location. Without any specific landmarks and no Global Positioning System, he couldn't determine his exact location.

"What are they?" Jorge asked, his eyes ping-ponging from Felix American Pony to Everrett "Mustache" Pacheco.

"One, have you seen that Steven Spielberg dinosaur movie and, two, do you know who Pablo Escobar is?" Mustache flicked his eyebrows in an almost comical manner.

"Are you serious?" Jorge's face scrunched up like a rotten, prickly pear.

"Read the room, Mustache," Felix said.

"Okay, okay," Mustache winced with a meme-worthy facial expression. "Um... I'll take that as a 'yes.' But, did you know Pablo Escobar had hippopotamuses?"

Jorge shook his head.

"You've seen the Joe Exotic documentary, right?" Mustache said. "About the private zoos?"

Jorge nodded.

"So, from that, we know that exotic and wild creatures have attracted men with less than admirable reputations," Mustache said.

That makes sense, Jorge thought. While expensive, reputable wildlife exhibits had been established in Presidio County, some eccentric wealthy individuals brought creatures like tigers and cheetahs. Exotics in this area weren't unprecedented either; he had personally almost hit a llama while driving along FM 170 East.

"You guys were dispatched to Big Bend State Park to hunt exotic animals?"

"*Exotic* is putting it lightly," Mustache said.

"We call them 'replicants,'" Felix American Pony interjected.

"Reh-?"

"Replicants," Felix repeated. "Look, I'm getting bored with just standing around talking. Can we at least hook you up with your armament."

"You're finally giving me back my gun?" Jorge snorted.

"Cut me some slack, Mondragon," Felix said, rolling his eyes. "You've done enough first responder training. You know if one of your bodies is knocked out that you're supposed to relieve 'em of their weapon before things go from bad to worse."

Jorge looked down at the ground and kicked at rocks with his boot.

"Not only will you get your weapons back, we're going to give you some of ours, *tambien,*" Mustache said.

"Feds?" Jorge said. "I already got a Glock."

Mustache shook his head, "Buddy, we ain't the Feds."

"Muy intersante," Jorge replied. His whole body grew warm with an almost sensuous heat as he thought of the possibility of weapons and ammunition.

Mustache slapped Jorge on the chest with the back of his hand, "C'mon, let's load you up on guns."

CHAPTER 12

The Gorgon

"It's a beautiful view," Tennyson said as the monster dragged him up the purple crater. "El Solitario."

Tennyson spoke with lacerated and burned lips from the journey. He had studied the map and pictures. Despite the physical trauma, he recognized that they had traveled through the waterway of Fresno Canyon and then northeast.

With ease, the Gorgon could yank its head left to right and break Tennyson's neck. Instead, with careful precision, it clamped the Californian in his mouth, how a mother would carry her offspring. The Gorgon's gargantuan size enabled it to cup the man in its mouth.

"He wants me alive," Tennyson surmised, his consciousness fading in and out. Both his internal and external temperatures were above one hundred degrees.

Unlike Brody, Tennyson didn't have a science background, and this was his first time in a "flyover state."

A while back, he'd visited his cousin in Florida. They'd spent time in the ocean and smoked marijuana. His cousin also had a Burmese python, but the last time he saw his cousin in Florida, that python was gone.

"Had to get rid of him, bruh," his cousin had said. "Too expensive."

"How much you get for him?" Tennyson had asked.

"Nada, man," he had said. "Had to let him go."

Tennyson hadn't thought much of that conversation—mainly because the levels of THC had distorted that particular visit. But afterward, he'd researched the Burmese python. People like his cousin released those creatures into the Florida ecosystem and created chaos. No natural predators for the Asian reptilian existed in the Floridian swamps, so its actions in the Everglades had gone unchecked. Entrepreneurs and conservationists had formed an uneasy alliance to thwart the ecological damage. Brave men and women wandered into the Everglades and worked to reduce the impact of the great snake.

"But Burmese pythons don't hunt humans," Tennyson said aloud, between his bruised and bloodied lips.

The negative impact of pythons on the Everglades' ecological system had yet to be determined. But with this creature, it was different. There was no variable. It had a definite, determined outcome. If this monster—

the great Gorgon synapsid—continued to live, it would terrorize life inside Big Bend.

Livestock and agriculture would be left in ruins. Generational ranches and farms would be destroyed. The monster's unchecked actions would crush the area's economy. This devastation would set the conditions for horrible outcomes. Desperation would breed temptations...

And the monster would continue to hunt.

"People will die."

CHAPTER 13

Jorge Mondragon

"Now, that is an ugly view," Jorge laughed as he stared at the rusted mobile home. "But it's also nice to know where I am."

Felix and Mustache led Jorge to an abandoned mobile home inside Big Bend State Park. From his time as a Park Police Officer, Jorge knew that they were now south of the Chorro Vista.

"Outside of it's pretty though," Mustache said.

"*Sí*," Jorge replied, looking at the desert succulents and purple wildflowers that ornated the rugged terrain and its enigmatic beauty. "But I'm kinda afraid Bryan Cranston is going to run out of that thing."

"Man," Felix shook his head, "I wish we were fighting against meth."

Mustache reached the mobile home first and pulled open the door. Jorge's gut tightened. On top of his recent concussion, he was now entering a mobile home with two complete strangers after hearing a story that didn't make any sense.

Jorge knew how to think with his gut. He knew he needed to follow his instincts, but new facts pushed him forward.

Jorge sighed.

"What's the matter?" Mustache asked.

"I guess that's all it takes," Jorge laughed.

"What's that?" Mustache asked.

"Guns," Jorge shrugged his shoulders.

"Guns?"

"For me to go into a weird place with strangers," Jorge shook his head.

"And apparently the only thing that makes you smile," Felix chided.

Mustache pointed inside, "We got Desert Eagles in there."

Jorge's whole face lit up. He felt an entire kaleidoscope of butterflies in his stomach. With light feet, he ascended the stairs.

Two men stood inside.

A tall, Hispanic man with salt-and-pepper hair dressed similar to his compatriots but with his blouse and kit removed. He had a shirt of synthetic materials, a distinct tiger tattoo on his right bicep, and "1824" inked into his forearm. Beside him stood a Caucasian man who didn't wear the military-inspired digital camouflage but duck hunting style, with a black trucker-style hat. The man in the trucker hat had blue nitrile gloves and cleaned the interior components of various weapon systems with an indescribable vigor.

"Howdy," the Hispanic man said.

"Hola," said the second.

Jorge twisted his mouth, fighting to conceal a smirk.

"So," Jorge crossed his arms, "you're the guys who are supposed to win me over?"

"You wanna see my Taurus Raging Bull?" the trucker-hat man said, holding up the black-and-chrome-handled revolver, modified with a black scope.

"Whatever you're up against feels like an excuse to procure the biggest, gimmicky guns possible," Jorge said.

"Let's just call it 'good targeting,'" Felix responded. "The right munition for the right problem."

"But," Mustache interjected, "these weapons are pretty cool. When you're staring down one of them nasty replicants, you gotta bring out the big guns, the real deal! Because of the creature's large size, even if you hit the heart, it will take a few minutes for a locomotion of its size to fall and for the blood to stop. And yes, the scopes on these overpowered pieces make sense too. You want those bullets hittin' the same spot, again and again, 'til that critter ain't movin' a muscle."

"Alright," Jorge said. "But what the heck is that?"

"This?" The man with the hat held up a long, black pole. "It's a shotgun stick. Also called an expendable shotgun with a customized 12-gauge magazine."

Jorge squinted as he looked at another contraption.

"Is that a..."

"Underbarrel Flamethrower?" The Hispanic man held up a Remington 870 DM with an under-barrel attachment.

"Um..." Jorge pointed to another weapon on the table. "I was pointing at that Russian piece right over there."

"Ah," the trucker-hat man picked up a black barrel, compact shotgun with a desert tan-colored forend and pistol-grip-only stock. "This is a KS-23... in our analysis, we didn't think we should put any attachments on it."

"Hang on," Felix held up both hands, "let's introduce these guys first."

"I think we're okay," the man in the trucker hat said.

Felix sighed. "The man with duck-legacy pattern clothes holding the KS-23 is Bill Bosworth. The team's design is based on the Special Forces Alpha Team model. While we don't have non-commissioned officers, he is our weapons subject matter expert. Spent his time as a hired gun in the sandbox, gettin' into trouble in Afghanistan and Iraq. Also served as a firearms instructor up in Oklahoma. He got big and famous in the Sooner State for developing a belt-style ranking system for his marksmanship school."

Bill Bosworth tipped his hat.

"The other man basically serves as the Team Sergeant. He served in the Marine Corps and then as Opfor down at Fort Polk, Louisiana. He retired and got into contracting."

"That *güey* over there's Geronimo?" Jorge asked.

"The most hated Battalion in the Army," Roy answered.

"He's a Texan *and* paratrooper," Jorge pointed at the 1824 tattoo on his forearm. "You should have introduced him to me first. What part of Texas?"

He slapped the 1824 tattoo, "San Antonio."

"Muy buen," Jorge said.

"Oh, and speaking of Texas," Bill pointed at Mustache. "Did he tell you we gave him his nickname?"

Jorge stared at Mustache, who grew red in embarrassment.

"We called him 'Valley Girl,' *porque* he's from McAllen. He grew out that 'stache and started calling himself that."

"Valley Girl?" Jorge laughed.

Mustache shook his head, "Mi padre always said: Friendship is beautiful but it ain't always pretty. Takin' grief from you douchebags ain't always fun."

"Well," Bill said, "I wouldn't call you pretty neither."

The group started to laugh, but BIA Agent Felix American Pony stepped.in.

"Alright, listen," Felix said. "We ain't got all day for you Texans to yammer on about Selena or the Alamo. You've seen the firepower. Let's get your gear together and I'll fill you in on what's ahead."

CHAPTER 14

Jorge Mondragon

Bureau of Indian Affairs Agent Felix American Pony handed the Texas Park Police Officer a white computer tablet. The men stood inside an airconditioned Big Bend Texas State Park mobile.

"Pero, I wanna look at the KG-23—"

"Here," Felix tucked the tablet in Jorge's hands. Jorge snorted and took the device.

Levity vanished. Jorge felt his stomach twist.

"Like I said," Felix tapped the screen. "They're called replicants. Remember that Spielberg flick? Well, there's some truth to it. You see, cloning from ancient bugs? That's just a fairy tale. But there's a guy, a paleontology expert, who says we can mess with modern DNA to bring back the old stuff. Ever heard of those 'dino-chicken embryos?' And the mammoths? Yeah, they're real, all right. Been making headlines—they're all over the mainstream news."

"Pero, what we're facing hasn't been reported on the media lapdogs," Jorge countered.

"And let me tell you," Felix leaned forward, his voice carrying a hint of frustration. "It ain't just about the science, you know. It's about power and fear. Those cartels? They're calling the shots."

"What?" Jorge scratched his head.

"Look, what Mustache was getting at with Pablo Escobar's hippos and Joe Exotic, it's all connected," Felix said. "Eccentric guys and cartel big shots have always had a thing for exotic critters. So, a replicant? It's the next natural step. Just think about it. Cartels got scientists and chemical engineers cooking up meth and building car batteries that do double duty. They even got their own submarines. You really think it's a stretch for them to tinker with the genetic code of, say, a mountain lion embryo?"

Felix reached over and swiped the screen. An artistic rendition of a Gorgonopsian Synapsid—the great saber-toothed synapsid—appeared.

"This," Jorge nodded at the computer screen, "is what killed *el chico*? Made my thousand-pound burro just disappear…without a trace? This is what haunts my park?"

Felix nodded.

"I originally thought cartels had carved up Enrique like that. I thought it would result in a 21st century border war. *Pero,* now I know the truth.

TERROR IN BIG BEND

A monster did this and because of its ties to the cartels, it will still potentially result in a second border war."

Felix nodded again.

"What the monster doesn't kill," Jorge clenched his teeth, "the war will."

36

CHAPTER 15

Jorge Mondragon

"It's not fair," Jorge shook his head and paced around the mobile home.

"What?" Felix laughed, his humor not harsh or painful but genuine shock.

"I know, I know," Jorge thumped his badge with a closed fist. "I'm supposed to be king of this area—Officer Mondragon, lord of Big Bend, *pero* I gotta be honest, Felix..."

Jorge felt the BIA agent's gaze soften. "Yes?"

"I'm tired, *amigo*. I've been on multiple deployments, and along the way, I convinced myself I couldn't do anything else. The truth is, I wanted to explore new things—start a family and get into agriculture, but tactics were the only thing I knew. I thought police work was the right transition, even though I had no real desire. I thought, being in the park, I could be alone, be isolated. Not necessarily free from danger, but free... from people."

Jorge stopped pacing and looked up at his audience—the band of men he had a complete ignorance of just three hours ago.

"Nope—it ain't fair at all," Felix shook his head. "We're really asking a whole heap from you."

Jorge's face scrunched in confusion. He hadn't known BIA Agent Felix American Pony for very long, but sympathy from him wasn't what he expected.

"Even though it's my duty?" Jorge asked.

"Your duty was to your soldiers, and you stood by them. You earned your rest, that's for sure. But," Felix added with a shake of his head, "it just ain't in the cards. I know you, Jorge—you ain't gonna sit back and rest—you won't let yourself do it."

"We might not all come back from this journey," Jorge said as he studied the faces of these strange men.

"I can't answer that," Felix said.

Mustache, who had appeared to be merry, so driven by his heart, now stood with an ashen face. Roy Raul looked downward, and apparent stress etched lines into his face. Bill Bosworth's light skin grew even more fair and his eyelids turned pink.

"*Pero*," Jorge returned to the tablet and picked it up. He pointed at the Gorgon, "I can't have this in my park."

As if in applause, Bill Bosworth racked the forend of the KS-23. Felix American Pony smiled, took the lethal instrument from him, and slung it around his chest.

"But impending doom doesn't mean you can't have a bit of fun," Bill Bosworth slapped the table, bringing Jorge's attention to the weapon-covered surface. Bill gave a broad smile, but the look of stress still remained. "Take your pick."

Jorge stepped forward. Jorge Mondragon had served as an M249 and M240B gunner in the infantry. As a law enforcement officer, he had certified in shotguns, patrol rifles, pistols, and numerous less-lethal devices. And because of that, his eyes rushed to the strangest instrument. He breathed in. His chest rose in reverence as he made his first selection.

"I choose you," he said to the weapon, grabbing the shotgun stick in both hands. He held the lance-like object above his head, angling to avoid flagging the other men.

Jorge smiled and slung the shotgun stick over his right shoulder. Next, he grabbed the Keltec KSG. Taking its sling and attached carabiner, he positioned it on his vest so the two shotguns didn't slam into one another. He grabbed a gold-colored Smith & Wesson XVR 460 Magnum and two revolver speed loaders.

"Good choice," Bill said.

Jorge laughed, "I ain't done yet."

Still laughing, the Park Police Officer grabbed a multitool and a black, tactical modern Kukri knife with subdued brass knuckles at its grip. He sheathed the melee weapon and then pulled it free.

"This task," Mustache said, "isn't what you wanted... heck, to tell you the truth, it ain't what any of us wanted. Maybe when this is all over..."

"*Olvídalo*," Jorge said, studying the blade. "I'll rest when I die."

CHAPTER 16

Jorge Mondragon

"*Chingado*," Jorge said, looking around the mobile home. "I'm not seeing a scenario where we just pack up and go get drunk in Ojinaga... are you?"

"Not a chance." Felix thought a moment. "And you?"

Felix watched Jorge sheath the knife, a bemused grin on his face. "I don't think the Mexican National Guard is gonna like you walking around with that Kukri. You know, Jorge, I think you might need us more than we need you."

"Want to fill me in on who you mean by 'we'?" It was less of a question than an attempt to change the subject. Jorge felt annoyed by Felix's prodding.

"Who's *we?*" Jorge demanded. "You're BIA, but what are they supposed to be? Spooks? Some three-letter group I ain't ever heard of?"

Felix let the silence hang. "Dark Waters."

Mercs.

Jorge's mouth dropped open as he stared at the other men in the small room. Mercenaries, known in professional sectors as security contractors, differed from how they had been presented in fiction. Between chasing deployments with the Guard, Jorge had done a few stints in security with the hopes of deploying with agencies like Dark Waters. But while he approved of the agencies, their clandestine patrols were in his area of responsibility.

"Dark Waters, huh?" Jorge's face twitched as he fought to stifle his anger. "You said something about the team's structure?"

"You got it," Felix said and grabbed his tablet again. "Influenced by the Army Special Forces Team."

The Bureau of Indian Affairs agent handed the tablet to Jorge.

"What are you showing me?" Jorge said, looking up at Felix and the other three men.

While Felix's face remained the same, Jorge saw the other men give awkward smiles, making evident their unease with sharing the content.

Must be classified, Jorge thought.

"That," Felix cleared his throat. "That's our team."

Jorge looked at the portable computer, "It's timed out."

"Yeah," Felix laughed, "this device is encrypted and will time out pretty quick."

Felix took the device, unlocked it, and returned it to him.

"We were put together because of our tactical backgrounds and command of the Spanish language," Roy said. "As a certain economy down south continued to crumble, oil companies needed to make sure that their personnel were able to safely escape."

"Makes sense," Jorge said, swiping his fingers down the glass.

"Then," Felix interjected, "we heard about Enrique Esparaza, the attack sounded like other intel reports I'd read. Myself, Hattori, and Gaxiola-Chicahua had been on a multinational task force working on... something else... but through that other operation, we have an understanding of the replicants. We know replicants needed more than one individual."

"So, we ain't fighting cartels?" Jorge asked.

"Our job is simple: kill the replicants in order to stop a war," Roy said.

"While shotguns are cool," Bill added, "if I'm fighting cartels, I'll take an AK over a shotgun."

"You mean an M4?" Jorge asked.

"Ha! I bleed red, white, and blue, but back when I was takin' on the Haj, it was always the trusty ol' Kalashnikov," Bill Bosworth said, the passion in his voice evident. "Here in the states, I'll flaunt my tricked-out AR-15 to my buddies, but when it comes to showin' off to my enemies, it's all about the AK."

Jorge dug his tongue into his mouth, stifling his mirth.

"A little forced?" Bill asked.

"Yeah... *un poquito.*"

"C'mon," Bill slapped Jorge on the shoulder, "I'll go show you what everyone carries."

From the corner of his eye, Jorge saw Felix roll his eyes and throw up his hands. "And can you introduce him to your team as well?"

CHAPTER 17

Jorge Mondragon

Jorge followed Bill outside. The two men exited the mobile home and walked back into Big Bend State Park. Jorge felt a little discomfort as he stepped out. From his infantry training, he knew to never gaggle. Enemy technology had the ability to pick up heat. In the last few decades, cameras had become even more prominent.

We're not hunting man, Jorge thought. *We're going after animals.*

And from Enrique's poor, tattered corpse, he knew the Gorgon relished the taste of human flesh. So, a mass of men in one area might draw the fiend nearer.

A picturesque figure of masculinity stood at the front of the line. The man stood six feet tall, with facial and follicle features that hinted at Puerto Rican ethnicity. The man wore the digital pattern of the unit, with his sleeves rolled up to his elbow, revealing thick muscles decorated with vascularity worthy of a muscle magazine. On his right forearm was the World War II Ranger Insignia—the blue diamond with the name in the center. Slung across his chest, he carried a Benelli M4, and on his hip was the oddly-shaped, Italian pistol, the Chiappa Rhino.

"I'm Jorge Mondragon," he offered his hand and forced himself to look away from the enigmatic massive revolver.

"Antonio Arzaga." The tall man removed his tactical gloves and extended his own hand. They shook, and when the iron grip closed around Jorge's hand, he knew at once that this man could break every one of Jorge's fingers if he so desired. Antonio must have seen it on Jorge's face because he offered a wolfish smile. "I got that name from *mi Mama*, but somewhere along the line, these mean brutes started calling me 'Gotham.' Just because I'm Nuyorican! But Mama didn't raise no crybaby. Sticks and stones, am I right, Jorge?"

"Definitely." The fact that Gotham had not released his hand made Jorge sense that this was a subtle laying down of the rules. If it was supposed to be a warning, Jorge could not decide. When Gotham released his hand, Jorge muttered, "Sticks and stones."

"I heard you were in the 1-143 here in Texas," Gotham said. "I was the Charlie Company Commander back in Rhode Island."

"Ay güey!" Jorge said. "We have three paratroopers."

"*Sí*, and not just five-jump-chumps, neither."

"Graduates of Airborne School are still paratroopers!" said a voice with an indescribable accent. A man of a similar stature to Gotham knelt beside a rucksack, conducting a meticulous inspection of a butterfly-coiled dry rope. Over his shoulder hung a KS-23. He had taken off his blouse and worked bare-chested. Tattoos ran from his right hand all the way up to his neck. Jorge recognized the Mountain Warfare insignia, an emblem unique to the National Guard. He also saw the enigmatic logo of the Floridian National Guard unit of the 53rd Infantry Brigade Combat Team.

"I never knew if that was a cosmonaut or a conquistador," Jorge pointed at the man's Florida National Guard tattoo.

"Ni," the man stood up and extended his hand. "It's a scuba diver."

"Really?"

The man laughed. "No, not really. It's to show Florida's Spanish history. I'm Tarzano Salvatore-Jones. I do the intelligence. Gotham and I both have the Ram's head, but to help him out, I carry the equipment. They already selected our team, but I had a side hustle in Florida hunting Burmese pythons and other exotics."

Ram's head was the vernacular term for the Army Mountain Warfare school in Jericho, Vermont. Regarding professionalism, Jorge now felt more confident traversing the rugged terrain.

"I'm Jimmy Martinez," the last man continued to cinch down his large, heavy backpack. "I was a Seabee in the Navy and serve as the Demolitions and Engineer for the team. I did a little bit of everything before going into contract work."

Jimmy stood up and sighed from the work he put into packing. He extended his hand for a fist pound. Jorge smiled and punched back.

"Does anyone know where Ben is?" Mustache asked.

"Who?" Jorge asked.

"Our treasurer," Mustache looked frustrated and scanned the area.

"I haven't seen him in a hot minute," Jimmy said.

Mustache sighed, "On his own program. Here—"

Mustache pointed at the two remaining men. One dressed in digital camouflage with the Japanese flag on his shoulder. He wore a professional tactical vest with a Velcro-nametape "Hattori" displayed on his chest.

"I'm Duke Hattori," the Japanese soldier said and extended his hand.

"Duke?" Jorge asked and scratched his head.

Duke laughed, "Yes, my father was a Japanese soldier trained by 1st Group out of Special Forces. I was named after him."

"Duke," Jorge felt his face scrunch like a prune. "Like John Wayne?"

"If you think that's crazy," Duke said, "wait 'til you meet this character."

Jorge looked past Tarzano at the last two men. One was the man he had seen earlier in the Mexican Army Uniform. His name tape read Gaxiola-Chicahua, but he didn't recognize the rank insignia.

"I'm Radames," the Mexican soldier said and extended his hand.

Jorge shook. *"Mi placer,"* Jorge said, smiling as he recognized the Mexican Army Parachutist badge on the man's uniform.

Suddenly, something slammed into Jorge's back. He jumped back. On instinct, he felt himself reaching toward his weapon.

"Whoa, whoa!" a man replied. He was dressed similarly to the rest of the Dark Waters, but Jorge didn't recognize him. Jorge—still filled with adrenaline from the surprise—breathed deeply, studying the man.

"Who," Jorge panted, "are—"

"You met our trickster," Mustache said and shook his head. "Where have you been?"

The man waved his hand, as if disregarding Mustache's concern.

"I'm Ben Andrade," the last man extended his hand to Jorge.

What the heck is wrong with you? Jorge continued to slow his breath.

Jorge sighed, "Last man on the team. *Encantado de conocerte."*

"Igualmente," Ben said, offering his hand. Jorge held out his hand, meaning to shake Ben's, but his eyes caught sight of something on Ben's palm instead.

Jorge froze.

Two black dots rested between Ben's thumb and forefinger. At first, Jorge thought they were tattoos, but they were too small. Not only that, they appeared to be jutting out ever so slightly from the skin of Ben's palm.

"Snake bite."

"What?" Jorge jerked away from Ben's outstretched hand to the man's face.

"It was a snake." Ben rubbed his finger over one of the dots, which were as black as oil. Jorge realized they were minuscule scars—almost unnoticeable to an oblivious eye. "I learned three things about snake charmers. One: those guys drain their cobra's venom packs before they have a show. Two: 'drained' does not mean empty. It bit me when I tried to pet it."

"What's the third thing?" Jorge asked, still staring at the two tiny black scars.

"That snake charmers chew on charcoal in case someone stupid tries to pet their snakes. He took my hand and spat charcoal into it. Absorbed enough of the poison to keep me from dying. Scarred over like that." Ben changed the subject. "I know what you're thinking."

"Oh yeah?" Jorge asked. "What's that?"

"You're thinking: *Why oh why did I let myself get dragged into this?* And you're probably thinking how the hell do I get away from these *locos.* How am I doing?"

Jorge broke eye contact with Ben. Was it that obvious? Ben said this with such confidence that Jorge felt his ugly thoughts were tattooed on his face or scarred into it like the bite mark on Ben's hand.

"Hey, look at me," Ben said, his voice soft. When Jorge looked at Ben again, there was no judgment in his face or mocking. "I'm thinking the same thing. I've been thinking it ever since I got here. It's okay."

Ben offered his hand. "I'm not as strong as Gotham. I promise I won't break your hand."

Jorge looked at Ben's hand and then shook it. The two black scars poked the flesh of Jorge's hand. It felt bizarre, feeling the two spots where Ben's life had almost ended, and all that had saved him was a mouthful of charcoal.

"Ben!" a voice called. "Can you get this GPS up and running?"

"Let me go check this out. Great meeting you." Ben patted Jorge on the arm and then ran to the problem.

Jorge watched him go. Ben's words had comforted him, but a chill crept up Jorge's spine. Ben's two black scars had prodded through the fabric of Jorge's shirt. For a brief instant, he pictured a snake biting him in the spot where Ben had patted him on the shoulder.

Jorge made a mental note to buy some charcoal.

CHAPTER 18

Jorge Mondragon

The harsh heat stung Jorge as he adjusted the straps on his rucksack, pulling the MOLLE tighter against his back. Big Bend State Park didn't have humidity but a dry heat that penetrated the whole body. Beside Jorge stood the Dark Water unit's leader, Antonio "Gotham" Arzaga. While Jorge worked, Ben Andrade ran past the two men and returned to his formation position.

"We back up and running?" Gotham asked as Ben ran past him and back into his formation.

"We're all good to go," Ben gave Gotham a thumbs up.

"They're all yours, Jorge," Gotham patted Jorge on the back.

Jorge smiled as he looked back at the men who followed him. While he had chosen Big Bend Park in an attempt to be away from people, sometimes he felt he needed more fellowship. Jorge still felt suspicious of the entire event and uncomfortable with the mystery of it, but his gut told him that these were good people.

Mustache's passion for people was an excellent counter to his grouchiness, and Felix American Pony seemed wise.

Heart. Mind. Technical knowledge. And his own reliance on intuition.

And you can't beat Bill Bosworth's selection of guns, he thought and looked down at the Keltec KSG slung across his torso.

Time had an interesting impact on Jorge. Yes, over the years, he had evolved into a grumpy old vet, but sometimes, something extraordinary happened and revived the idealism of his youth. As a seasoned trigger puller and lawman, he made most decisions with his gut, but it was nice to use his heart.

First, it was the cat. Mr. Gato's instant affection for him had revived parts of his passionate past. Jorge had been a three-time volunteer: volunteering to enlist in the Texas National Guard, attending Airborne School, and volunteering to deploy. These men had followed a similar path. Impending peril threatened them, but a sense of duty drove them forward.

Jorge laughed to himself, *Except, of course, Brody. What the heck is that surfer dude doing out here?*

Felix and the others decided that the best course of action was for hippie and former *alleged*-doctor-of-veterinary-science to come along on their journey. Time dictated an immediate pursuit of Brody's friend Tennyson. Brody had seen the monster and knew his friend.

Big Bend was no joke. It was the most beautiful park in Texas, but dangerous. Seven species of venomous snakes slithered through the area. Black bears with the strength of five men foraged the site, and the great American mountain lion called the park home.

And if the predatory fauna didn't kill Brody, the flora might. The yuccas, candelillas, and sotol, though possessing a strange and alluring beauty, could penetrate through clothing and lacerate human flesh. In attempts to avoid the mesquite trees, hikers would make minor adjustments. When the daylight faded, those small adjustments would turn into circles, resulting in hikers becoming disoriented and lost.

Brody would have been too great of a liability to let him walk back through the rugged terrain by himself.

And now he's just an operational liability.

Jorge laughed and shook his head to better focus on the mission. The operation consisted of two key tasks:

- Find the monster
- Kill it

Simple enough.

While they hunted the Gorgon and not the men, the collective tactical background of the group forced them into a wedge formation. Jorge would serve as a point man for the direction of travel as he followed the monster's footprints. Jorge knelt on the ground. Gotham crept forward, close enough that his leg pressed against Jorge's rucksack, and scanned the area, looking for any potential threats as Jorge investigated.

Jorge's eyes lit up as he studied the sediments. He angled his head, looking for any evidence of the monster.

"Gotcha," Jorge snapped with his soft fingers as he saw the Gorgon's impression on the ground. He stood up and Gotham moved back to his position. Jorge said nothing, but turned to the tall man and nodded. He then started walking. From the corner of his eye, Jorge saw Gotham wave his unit forward as Jorge followed the sign.

CHAPTER 19

The Gorgon

The Gorgon dropped Tennyson. He lay flat against the ground and covered his head with his hands. Tennyson closed his eyes. The Gorgon growled over him. A globulous drip of saliva covered Tennyson's head. Microtremors shook underneath him. He tilted his head sideways and, summoning all his courage, opened one eye.

The monster walked away. Despite the muscularity that clung to the monster's skeletal frame, it moved forward with cat-like grace.

"Great," Tennyson spat loose grains of sand from his mouth. "He's letting me live."

Tennyson groaned as he got on all fours and struggled to stand. The sun shone on his exposed, lacerated legs where the soil had torn through his jeans. Solar rays seared the pink, vulnerable flesh.

"If I survive this," he said, "I'll still die of skin cancer."

Tennyson braced himself against the side of the volcano and watched the hind feet of the Gorgon as it walked away. He stretched his neck, trying to spy on the monster.

The Gorgon then stopped. With swift and silent precision, it turned. Tennyson slammed against the ground as fear consumed him and his body failed. Tennyson's head bounced against a copper-colored rock. Blood seeped from his eyebrow. He lay flat against the sand. But while his limbs and bowels failed him, and now blood hindered his view, he could still see.

In a motion similar to a house cat, the Gorgon went in multiple cycles before letting itself slam into the sand. Then relaxing all its muscles, it lay on the desert floor. Tennyson's lungs beat against the ground as he panted in shallow, excited breaths. While he struggled for air, he still watched.

The primordial fiend's protruded and engorged belly raised up and down in slow rhythmic patterns. It traced its tongue on its saber teeth. Tennyson moved at a snail's pace to his knees.

"It's sleeping?" Tennyson scratched his head. "An after-meal nap?"

A sudden and unexpected rage gripped the man. This titan, which had inflicted so much physical and psychological trauma, found Tennyson to be of no threat at all. It didn't even attempt to conceal itself.

Can animals feel contempt? Tennyson thought.

It wasn't as if the Gorgon was challenging him. No, it didn't even consider Tennyson a potential annoyance.

Gritting his teeth, he reached down and grabbed a rock. The monster was right, Tennyson wasn't a mortal threat, but maybe, with his dying efforts, he could inflict some form of pain. He breathed in and out through gritted teeth and shambled forward. Perhaps he could slam the rock in the Gorgon's eyes or genitals—one final act of defiance before his demise.

But then something distracted him. A scent shocked his nose.

"Do I smell..." he tilted his head back and sniffed the air. "Gasoline?"

Between the pain and his use of narcotics, Tennyson doubted his current sensory situation. Dropping the rock, he raised his hands, shading his eyes as he scanned the area.

"We're still in El Solitario."

He had wished to see the great volcano but never thought it'd be his final resting place. His knees grew weak as he thought of his impending death.

Will this be my final resting place? He shuddered as he thought of what would happen to his body after being consumed by the Gorgon.

But while the thoughts of his own mortality threatened to push him into an existential crisis, his senses still confused him.

"I *do* smell gasoline."

Tennyson hobbled forward, attempting to follow the scent. He looked down at his wrist; his watch—though damaged—still worked. Mud caked the screen. He spat on its face and rubbed it. He then set the timer for twenty minutes.

"Alright," he said, "let's go explore."

Hobbling on his pain-filled legs, he moved. While his body shook, he managed to keep his balance as he walked past the great Gorgon. Starting from its rear, he saw the tail whipped back and forth in sleep. Its hind and front legs were about five feet long with horrible claws. Its paws were also semi-feline in appearance, with terrible, yellow nails extending from them. While it slept, it made no noise, but Tennyson's stomach churned at the thing's ability to remain silent.

Across its body, stubbly, proto-mammalian whisps of black whiskers covered its walrus-like skin. Its snout and whiskers wiggled back and forth. But while the motion appeared almost humorous, the bits of entrails and other unidentified pieces of gore that ornated the whiskers dampened any levity in the situation. As the Gorgon slept, it flexed its front claws, and as it did, the yellow nails retracted and extended.

Tennyson continued walking. He was unsure if courage motivated him forward or if a new-found indifference to his impending end enabled him. He passed the monster and increased his pace.

As he walked, the smell grew stronger. Tennyson looked down at his watch. He had been walking now for ten minutes. The growing smell now had him convinced he wasn't hallucinating. No longer did he smell only gasoline but also burning plastics. Bits of metal and other debris polluted the side of the volcano. A pair of faux leather-covered seats added more colors to the chaos. Rocks and other sediments lay scattered around the area from the evident impact.

"I've found where the smell is coming from," he said. "But now, I really think I'm crazy."

A heavily damaged airplane lay discarded against the side of El Solitario.

CHAPTER 20

Tennyson

Tennyson pressed his hands up against the side of El Solitario. Pain shot through him as he looked back at the Gorgon. It lounged, with what Tennyson treated as complete indifference. Its engorged belly rose up and down. Rage shook him and he had to turn his face away from the monster or the emotion would consume him.

"Focus on the plane," he said aloud.

He turned his head and spied the broken vessel. Pain shook from his busted legs through the rest of his body as he walked to the plane. At the rear of the aircraft, the ramp lay fallen out like the rotting tongue of an opened-mouth roadkill corpse.

Morbid curiosity pushed him forward. With dragging feet, Tennyson stepped inside.

He cursed, grabbed the bottom of his shirt, and covered his mouth. A business of flies buzzed through the gore-stained compartment. The back of the destroyed 727 remained relatively intact. The inside of the aircraft didn't look like the inside of a commercial plane, but a customized cargo. It reminded Tennyson of the pictures of paratroopers from World War II, but without the forty soldiers jammed into the area. Footprints, identical to the Gorgon from dusty substances, were pressed against the floor. Once inside, he took the pressure off his lower body by pushing against the side of the wall, then hand-over-hand, and in coordination with his feet, he crept forward. In an awkward fashion, Tennyson tilted his head bent upward, fighting to keep his mouth covered and hoping to muffle the smell.

Looking around the plane's rear, he realized the damage wasn't just from the external blows.

Something happened back here too.

The walls pressed outward. The same terrible print—the giant sign of the Gorgon—smashed into the side of the walls. Pieces of equipment were torn asunder as if caught on the monster's paws as it tried to pull away.

He winced as the spatter of blood decorated the craft; the business of flies rested on it, sucking at the scarlet stain. The portholes were broken inside the vessel, with the cracked glass pointing outward.

No blood there, though.

Tennyson's mind rushed back to the monster. The entirety of the 30-foot beast was covered in epidermis, similar to a rhinoceros. On the terrible journey to the volcano, its paws smashed through an ocotillo. Tennyson had screamed out in pain as the thorny spine-covered stems dug into his flesh and ripped apart his pajama bottoms. No cries, no wince, or other sounds came from the Gorgon as it plowed through the painful plant. Its massive paws smashed through the magenta opuntia macrocentra with no demonstration of pain.

What could make that thing bleed?

Tennyson scratched his head. He had been enamored with marijuana since high school. He had even given up his academic endeavors to focus on its consumption. The junior Earth Liberation Front was one of the few activities he had ever joined during his academic career. The school club had protested outside the house of a dentist who had hunted big game in Africa. While Tennyson knew little about weapons or ammunition, many of their ELF adult mentors were knowledgeable and had told him to penetrate the skin of elephants, it required special shotguns called "elephant guns." Weapons that were even more potent than a rifle or twelve gauges.

Or had it been physics? The combination of 747's speed and the rough, invulnerable surface of El Solitario? Could a pachyderm survive a plane crash? Even if he hadn't been so engrossed in the ingestion of hashish, he was pretty sure that had not been a subject studied in biology class.

Tennyson screamed out in agony as a sharp, excruciating pain shot through his foot, pulling him from his thoughts. He looked down. A jagged, protruding puncture pushed through the plane. He had stepped on it.

He cursed violently and stepped back. With careful precision, he balanced backward, pulling his lacerated foot free from the object. His demolished shoe clung to the obstacle.

"Oh, no!" Tennyson cried. A mass of dried blood painted the twisted metal in a glistening, dark purple.

His stomach churned. He had just had a blood transfusion with a monster.

Tennyson knew about the Human Immunodeficiency Virus to remember that it had originated from Belgian Congo chimpanzees. Research suggested the disease's genesis came from the transmission of infected primate blood to man.

What prehistoric prions now danced through Tennyson's blood cells? What horrible zoonotic disease would originate in his body?

Involuntary tears now sprang from his eyes. Despite his dehydration, the extreme emotion forced gobs of saliva to form in his mouth as he sobbed. Blood-sized drops of sweat covered his head.

"I can't afford to sweat," he sniveled, wiping the tears from his face.

Suddenly, a voice cried out: *"Quién está ahí?"*

Tennyson's whole body shook. Then, the tears stopped. He wiped at a string of mucus that hung from his nose.

"H-h-hello?" he managed with a snot-congested throat.

"Estoy aqui!" a pitiful voice answered. *"Estoy aqui!"*

Whether misguided or not, a burst of hope ran through Tennyson. It alleviated the sadness in his brain and provided much-needed energy to his body. Despite the overwhelming trauma, Tennyson shuffled forward. He no longer used his hands but pushed ahead with horrible, shabby steps.

"Estoy aqui!"

There at the front, was a closed door to the cockpit. The stranger cried out again from behind the cockpit door.

"I'm coming!" Tennyson pushed forward. "I'm coming!"

Then, with all his remaining energy, he shoved the door open and fell forward, past the door, and smashed into the floor.

CHAPTER 21

Tennyson

Tennyson struggled to his knees in the wrecked cockpit. Bits of the Big Bend Volcano—rock and cacti—spilled into the pilot's area. Tennyson groaned as he pressed against the destroyed navigation vessels to assist himself in standing up.

"Agua," the stranger's voice cried, *"agua."*

Tennyson turned to the noise. A man sat pinned to his steering wheel. The aviator was bent at the waist, his upper body hanging over the wheel. The aviator had long, black and gray shoulder-length hair and a black leather vest that had "A380" with the shape of a plane beautifully stitched into the back with an intimidating scarlet thread.

Tennyson felt excitement in the presence of another human, but something about the man also filled him with fear. Tennyson had pursued sensory-enhanced experiences but never studied the "gut." He couldn't quite articulate why he felt uncomfortable. Beautifully-crafted tattoos covered the man's arms with vibrant colors, with images of a man with a pronounced forehead and finely groomed mustache with the name *"Malverde"* printed underneath. On the dying man's exposed, muscle-bound tricep, an image of a skeleton, similar to the grim reaper with the name *"Santa Muerte,"* ornated his olive-colored flesh. Tennyson had spent all his adult life around drug dealers, but this man was different. This man, despite his vulnerable state, struck Tennyson with terror.

An odd emotional combination—pity and fear.

"Can you speak English?" Tennyson asked.

The long-haired man nodded, "Yes, I studied your language."

Tennyson's eyes bulged from his skull, shocked by the man's clear pronunciation of each syllable. The man's voice sounded similar to a news anchor while there was still a throaty growl from his evident agony.

"Your English is great."

"Yes, I had to study English to become a pilot," he managed.

"W-w-what happened here?" Tennyson stuttered as the terror returned.

The man reached out his hand. Tennyson trembled in fear. The man waved him forward. Tennyson's mind grew confused. He stepped back and his eyes swelled as he looked at the man.

"You must believe me," the man said.

"Believe what?"

"That we didn't do this. The cartels don't conduct hits on this side... they got free."

"Free... wait, what do you mean by 'they?'"

"He hit us. Brought me down, they got loose."

"What is they?" Tennyson said.

"The exotics—"

"Wait!" Tennyson cried. "There's more than one?"

The man stopped and spoke in Spanish, closing his eyes in obvious pain.

"The man who never speaks," the cartel aviator shook his head in disgust. "He found me, walked right up to me."

"Who are you talking about?"

The aviator coughed up blood and broken teeth, painting his broken electrical devices with bits of gore.

"He should have tortured me, you know? Like a decent criminal..."

Tennyson crept forward and placed his hand on the dying man's shoulder. He sensed this man's mortality fading. Never before had Tennyson been so moved with concern for others, but he knew he had to work.

"You gotta help me. We gotta tell the world what happened here," Tennyson cried.

"Yes!" the man coughed blood again. "These exotics *here,* running loose? That'll do it."

Tennyson's face stretched with a frozen, fake smile as he patted the man on the back and tried to console his pain. But while he intended to be like a parent comforting a grieving or sick child, he looked more like a child giving an artificial embrace to a sibling.

"El Diablo con una boina y pintura facial blanca!"

"The monsters, you gotta tell me about them," Tennyson begged. "What is out there?"

"Just stood there, *haciendo muecas*! *No hablaba!"* The aviator spat.

Tennyson scratched his head.

"There are dinosaurs out there!" Tennyson yelled. "How do I kill them?"

"*Sí*," the man whispered.

"They came from this plane, right? You crashed the plane and they got out! How do we stop them?"

The aviator laughed, "That's what I'm trying to tell you."

"I'm asking about dinosaurs, and you're talking about just *one man!"* Tennyson winced as his physical pain returned.

"Yes! He must have found out our specified route."

"What does that even mean?"

The man closed his eyes.

"No, no, no, no!" Tennyson drove past any remaining fear and shook the man. "Help me!"

The man must have understood Tennyson's desire. He opened his eyes and nodded.

"The man. He knew we were coming. He shot us down!"

"What?" Tennyson screamed. "That makes no sense. Why would anyone do that? Cartels keep that stuff down south, right?"

The man nodded, "Yes."

"Then why? Why did he shoot you down?"

"Como una brona."

"What? I-I don't. Who! Who did this?"

The man nodded. He closed his eyes and breathed in as if trying to garner strength. He shuttered. But while injuries plagued the man, somehow Tennyson knew it wasn't related to any physical trauma.

"Please," Tennyson whispered. "Tell me who."

"El Mimo."

CHAPTER 22

Jorge Mondragon

Jorge and the group hiked through Big Bend State Park. Sweat drenched Jorge's Park Police Officer uniform. He grimaced while his mind rushed to bitter-sweet memories. The rough material of his pants scratched the inner skin of his tender thighs. While the coarse cloth irritated his flesh, it reminded Jorge of past hikes and ruck marches.

The good old days, he thought.

Of course, he wasn't sure what that meant. He was curious to know if anyone knew what that phrase meant. His training and experience in the military did have some good times. Still, he also had some miserable times and had destroyed his knees, shoulders, and temperament.

In fact, his time in the service had left him longing to be alone, and as a result, he had taken the job in Big Bend in his pursuit of isolation.

Pero, truth be told, Jorge thought to himself. *It ain't good for a man to be alone.*

He looked behind him and saw Mustache, then turned to Bill. Now, he didn't want to be crammed into a community shower or stand naked in a long line waiting for his Bicillin injection, aka the Peanut Butter shot, but being around people wasn't bad.

Being around good dudes, that is, he thought.

However, Jorge wasn't going to tell them that.

The monster could move in complete silence and strike at will. While stealth characterized the Gorgon, its mass created a distinct trail. Jorge had been able to follow both the low sign of the footprints that misplaced rocks and the high sign of the destroyed vegetation.

In the hours of walking, Jorge had found relief in the form of Bureau of Indian Affairs Agent Felix American Pony. Before transferring to the BIA, the government unit's leader had served in the Shadow Wolves with ICE. But while Felix was a skilled tracker, Jorge knew Big Bend and its response to nature. Felix had worked in the Sonoran Desert, and Jorge here, in the Chihuahuan Desert.

"That's weird," Jorge whispered to himself. He held up his hand, balling it into a fist—signaling the group to halt.

Gotham, the leader of the Dark Waters unit, ran to Jorge's side.

"What you got?"

"That thing's sign," Jorge pointed at the hard-packed gravel. "It's doing something weird—like dragging something against the surface.

It's called brushing out; *contrabandistas* do it all the time... but, an animal?"

Jorge stroked his chin. Bile crept up his throat. A nauseating feeling gripped him.

"I think I figured it out," he whispered.

Gotham, hearing Jorge's whispers, leaned toward him.

"The creature is dragging Brody's friend in its mouth."

"You can tell all that by looking at the dirt?" Gotham pulled his eyes from security and stared at Jorge with a gaping jaw and swollen eyes.

"Prints tell you a lot."

"Is he dead?"

"I don't think so. Look," Jorge pointed at marks in the sand. "Every once in a while you will see a soup can. They're about every twenty yards or so. If he was dead, it would only be the brush out."

"Soup can?"

"Sorry. That is a jargon term for a specific type of shoe print," Jorge explained. "Popular with hipsters, and if he's anything like the other 'brah' in our group, he probably wears shoes like that."

Gotham scratched his head, "You can tell that from the dirt?"

"Should we tell Brody about the sign?" Jorge asked, studying the ground.

"I've seen paratroopers get knocked out and dragged across the drop zone," Gotham said. "They get second degree burns, so if Brody's friend ain't dead right now, he's probably wishing he was.... Jorge?"

Jorge now lay prostrate on the ground, angling his head. Then, he jumped to his feet and sprinted twenty feet forward. He stopped and pulled his binoculars from his vest.

"Gotham!" Jorge yelled over his shoulder.

"What's up?"

"Get Mustache," Jorge lowered the binos and stared at Gotham. "We're going to need a medic."

CHAPTER 23

Jorge Mondragon

"I just wanted to be left alone," Jorge muttered as he stared at the object in Big Bend State Park. *"Pero* looks like there's other plans."

Jorge sprinted forward. He inclined his torso forward and his hands swung back and forth with the characteristics of a trained sprinter. Dust shot high in the air behind him.

A shimmering, slime-coated mess lay in the beige soil next to a cactus. Under the globulous material lay a maimed and twisted man. Jorge winced. As Jorge studied the man, it appeared the nexus of the man's agony was the exposed vertebrae that punctured the bruised flesh.

"Qué pasa?" Jorge asked as he put on black tactical gloves. He set his hand on the man's shoulder.

"No toques!" The saliva-covered man coughed.

Jorge pulled his hand back and stared at the man.

"What happened…"

While the dying man spoke, Jorge focused on his hand. The glove felt as if it had increased in temperature. Jorge yanked off the glove, letting it fall to the ground. He stared in horror as smoke rose from the soiled object and it sizzled.

It's burning.

Jorge turned back to the man.

That man is covered in some sort of acid.

The man—his overwhelming pain evident—grew calm as his face and relaxed eyes grew dull. The man flexed his lips, working to speak.

Jorge stared at the carnage before him, trying to lean near the man but not wanting to be burned. He careened his neck forward.

"Ma-tay-yuh-may," the victim croaked.

The man lifted his head slightly, *"Mátame."*

Jorge's eyes bulged. He knew what the man was trying to say:

Kill me.

CHAPTER 24

Jorge Mondragon

Jorge fell backward, landing in a sitting position. The hot sand of the Chihuahuan Desert burned through his pants.

"Mátame," the victim repeated.

Jorge's body language remained strong; besides sitting, there was no visible weakness. But despite the Park Police Officer's masculine exterior, tears swelled in his eyes.

"I can't mercy kill…."

Before he could finish, Mustache bounded forward. Jorge could hear Mustache's fast and heavy footfalls, even over his tinnitus.

But as he ran, his feet dragged. His right foot caught on the cactus. Mustache catapulted skyward. His body went up and down.

WHAAM!

Mustache slammed into the acid-soaked man.

"No!" Jorge cried, "Please no!"

Mustache rolled off the man. He got onto his hands and knees and tried to push off the ground. But his wrist gave way; he stumbled over. His face smacked into the man's chest.

Mustache rolled over and screamed. His cries started in a horrible baritone, then reached a high tenor. The screams evolved into spit-filled gurgles.

Jorge ripped off his shirt to cover his hands and perform chest compressions.

But it was too late.

When Mustache sucked in the air to scream, he inhaled acid into his lungs and mouth.

Smoke rose skyward from Mustache's nose and mouth.

Jorge yanked off his own vest and threw it on Mustache's stomach. With his hands covered in cloth, he pounded his hands against Mustache's heart.

Jorge's eyes dilated in intensity as he focused on reviving his friend.

"Jorge, what do you need?" Gotham's voice cried out behind him.

Jorge didn't look up, but out of the corner of his eye, he saw the Dark Waters leader sprinting.

"Check his pulse!" Jorge yelled, his voice amplified by the chaos and by his own adrenaline. "But don't touch his face or hands! He's covered in acid!"

Gotham said something inaudible to Jorge as he continued chest compressions. Jorge worked, and through peripheral vision, he saw Gotham digging through Mustache's pants, feeling his legs and searching for a pulse.

"C'mon, Mustache!" Jorge yelled. "Don't die on me!"

Gotham stopped and stood up. The Dark Waters leader placed his hand on Jorge's shoulder.

"Jorge," Gotham whispered.

Jorge heard his name but ignored it.

"You can stop," Gotham said.

"*Callate!*" Jorge continued compressions.

"He's gone," Gotham said.

Jorge shook his head, still pushing.

"Jorge!" Gotham shouted.

Jorge let his eyes wander as he pressed. Mustache's now-deformed face lay sideways. Smoke rose from the melting features.

"He's gone," Gotham whispered.

Jorge fell sideways, avoiding the burning chemicals.

"What... what does that mean?" Jorge asked.

He wasn't sure why he asked the question. He surmised he couldn't stop if there was still hope. He felt Gotham's concerned look. He wanted to continue chest compressions. Despite his question, Jorge knew what Gotham meant and couldn't accept it.

He knew Mustache was dead.

CHAPTER 25

Jorge Mondragon

Jorge stood slack-jawed, staring at the Cronenberg-esque scene before him in the hot Chihuahuan desert. Gore polluted the gravel-covered terrain with flecks of unidentifiable tissue.

"I… I really liked Mustache" Jorge said.

"What do we do now?" a voice said.

Jorge turned to see Ben Andrade, *"Que?"*

"With the body."

Jorge balled his fists, ready to fight.

"Stop!" another voice rang out.

Jorge bared his teeth.

Gotham jumped in between the two men and Felix followed suit.

"That *body* was Mustache!" Jorge yelled and gesticulated with evident indignance.

Jorge's fingers twitched. Gotham set his hand on Jorge's shoulder.

"He was the first guy to make me laugh since Enrique died!" Jorge spat.

Jorge saw Felix creeping closer to Ben.

"I think he meant the first victim," Gotham whispered, wrapping a powerful arm around Jorge's shoulder.

"No," Jorge shook his head and stared at Ben. "He did not."

Ben paused. His face remained still, but his eyes twitched to Gotham and then back to Jorge.

"What?" Ben exclaimed. "Mustache was my friend! Are you insane?"

Jorge felt the blood rush from his face.

"I was asking an operational question about the first victim," Ben said.

"What do you mean?" Jorge asked, avoiding eye contact as he felt himself blushing.

"You ever hear of a baited ambush?" Ben asked.

Now, Jorge felt stupid and avoided eye contact.

"Ah," Gotham snapped his finger. "Perfected by Genghis Khan."

"I know what a baited ambush is!" Jorge spat.

"Whoa!" Ben held up both hands. "I just meant we could conserve energy… so we could properly pay respect to Everrett."

Jorge's nose wrinkled up, unfamiliar with the name.

"Everrett Pacheco?" Ben shook his head. "Mustache?"

61

I forgot his name, Jorge thought, then looked at the ground and kicked at rocks.

"We have to find Tennyson!" another voice cried out. Jorge turned to see Brody running toward them.

Bring in the clowns, he thought.

"My friend!" Brody pointed a trembling finger at the great Bofecillos Mountains. "My friend is up there!"

Jorge cast a glance at Gotham.

"Brody," Jorge started.

"Wait," Ben held a finger up. "We're designed after Green Berets; we can do both."

"What?" Jorge asked.

"We have to take care of Mustache," Gotham said. "But while we can be reverent, we can also be shrewd."

Jorge turned his slitted eyes at Gotham, then to Ben.

"We preserve Mustache's body, but allow the scent to linger in hopes of drawing the Gorgon close."

Jorge ground his teeth so hard pain shot through his jaws.

"If we try and take Everrett back right now," Gotham said, "we wouldn't be prepared. That monster knocked over your truck. We would be taking both back. We'd be exhausted. We'd be easy prey."

Jorge relaxed his muscles.

"We could protect ourselves and Everrett."

"Alright," Felix stepped toward the center of the group. "Sounds like we got ourselves a plan that just might work. Let's get some 360 security going and nail down the details."

CHAPTER 26

Jorge Mondragon

"You don't think things will get a little too complicated?" Jorge asked as he knelt beside the makeshift planning bay on the Big Bend State Park desert floor. It was what the Army called a "sand table kit," using the terrain and vegetation around the Big Bend State Park. Tarzano, Jimmy Martinez, Radames Gaxiola-Chicahua, and Duke Hattori built models out of the dirt to show their location, then used their identification cards to represent the individual.

"We're designed to be able to split up," Gotham said.

"We'll have all the G-men: myself, Duke Hattori, and Radames Gaxiola-Chicahua stay with the ambush. That way each group has a sign-cutter and a leader."

"Where am I going?" Jorge asked.

Felix sighed. "This ain't easy. Being as I'm the leader, I was always taught to go with the main effort—"

"Pero the park is *mio,* Felix," Jorge said. "You've done your duty."

"Then Jorge is still following Tennyson?" Brody interjected.

Jorge scratched his head at the hippie's zeal.

"Yes," Felix said.

"I'm going with him."

Jorge shook his head, "It's time I move hard and fast, Brody—"

"I'll keep up," Brody interrupted.

"You're outta your league," Jorge said. "This ain't no 'shroom induced walk through the park…."

"He saved your life," Gotham interjected. "I'd say he's earned his Stetson."

"Well, I ain't no cav scout!" Jorge countered.

"I'm going with you!" Brody said. "And not because anyone gave me their approval. I know Tennyson, and I have a background in animal science!"

Jorge couldn't conceal his contempt as he rolled his eyes.

This dead-head will get me killed, he thought as he kicked at rocks.

"Fine," Jorge said. "Let's finish the plan."

CHAPTER 27

Jorge Mondragon

After two hours of deliberation, the teams were set.

Dark Waters Team Alpha consisted of Gotham as Team Leader and Jorge on sign. Brody went with Jorge due to his knowledge of Tennyson and his alleged veterinarian background. Bill Bosworth, the team's weapons expert, went with the moving element. This left the ambush team needing its weapon expert to help lay in, but efforts were made to mitigate that risk. Tarzano, with his expertise in climbing, would also go with the moving element.

Dark Waters Team Bravo had been designed to lure the Gorgon into an ambush. They were also given the task of preserving the two victims' corpses.

Roy Raul would serve as the Dark Waters Team Leader and the weapons expert. Because the official weapons expert went with Alpha, the Demolitions Expert, Jimmy Martinez, would help build the ambush with explosives. Rounding out the Dark Waters Team Bravo was Ben Andrade, who could better relay all communications from remaining in a more static position. Furthermore, his knowledge of snakes (as seen from his bites) helped Bravo mitigate the risk of the Trans-Pecos copper head, Mojave Rattlesnake, and other venomous snakes that slithered through Big Bend.

All the members of Government representatives—Felix American Pony, Duke Hattori, and Radames Gaxiola-Chicahua, would serve with Dark Waters Team Bravo.

Special consideration had to be taken due to the environment. The Gorgonopsian Synapsid replicant had created radical change to the Big Bend ecological infrastructure. Both flora and fauna would respond in atypical ways. It was predicted that the Gorgon's large size could create rockslides that could form sediment avalanches.

From analysis, it was determined that explosives needed to be used to immobilize the Gorgon, synchronized with well-aimed shots of shotgun slugs to kill it.

After finalizing the plan, the two teams ate, hydrated, reset, and sorted equipment before they departed.

PART III

"Damned be the dark ends of the earth where old horrors live again." –
Robert E. Howard

CHAPTER 28

Felix American Pony

Felix American Pony stood on the mountain overlooking Fresno Canyon in Big Bend State Park. The canyon was north of FM 170 Road. From the mountain, a twisted polypropylene rope stretched down to the ground.

The BIA agent held his binoculars to his eyes. Drops of sweat landed on the glass, obscuring his view.

"Dry heat," he muttered to himself. It had been a few years since Felix had spent time in the desert. Not since he had served with the Shadow Wolves, hiking over the Quinlan and Baboquivari Mountains. Most recently, he and Duke Hattori had been assigned to Kaw City, Oklahoma. While the Sooner State had heat, it was a humid heat. Both were dangerous, but humidity at least made it easy to sweat. Dry heat attacked the whole body.

He dried his face with his bandana and looked through the spectacles. Looking down in Fresno Canyon's dried-out riverbed, he could see heat waves rising. As Ben covered and hid the corpses, Jimmy Martinez set in explosives.

He lined parts of the canyon's walls with the combustible components. With expert precision, the former Seabee angled the combustibles downward. This increased the lethality of the blast by enabling bits of the limestone on the sheer vertical walls to act as additional pellets.

"That man volunteers for the jobs I don't want," Felix said as he studied Ben with his binoculars. Earlier in the mission, they had driven to Presidio County. En route, traveling along the twisting roads, they hit a beautiful Golden Retriever.

The animal had torn at their hearts with its dying whimpers. It had to be put out of its misery.

As a leader, Felix felt responsible for taking unnecessary tasks like that from his men, so they'd be better. But Ben had volunteered to do it. Heck, he had volunteered to take care of these bodies too.

Weird thing, Felix thought, *Ben ain't afraid to get his hands dirty with the dead stuff. Turns out, that might just work in our favor.*

Felix winced, realizing what he had just thought. He took another glance at the treasurer. As part of the contract for the Dark Waters to get this mission, all had to pass background investigations, which included a polygraph.

Felix had personally administered the team's tests. Out of the entire team, Ben had done the best. And, he had a solid recommendation from his time with the Center for Disease Control.

"Hmmm," Felix shook his head, refocusing his energies on scanning the area.

He cursed in amazement. A trail of dust rose into the air. In the Sonoran Desert, Felix had seen dust devils. But while they traveled in a circular tornado-like motion, this did not travel like that.

"Something is running!" Ben yelled.

The others around him screamed up at him.

That's it, Felix thought.

Felix's knees shook. A Gorgonopsian Synapsid sprinted their way. Its motion was identical to a feline. Its front paws struck the ground—left then right—its hind legs followed the pattern. Black orbs stared in shock; their mouths gaped open. A tremendous black tongue hung from its side.

"Everyone in position!" Felix yelled.

The initial plan involved the animal chasing the scent and hunting. Felix leveled his shotgun and scratched his head with his non-firing hand.

"That thing ain't hunting!" Felix yelled. "It's in a dead sprint!"

But that wasn't accurate either.

No, the monster ran zig-zagging in an indescribable pattern, with a lolling tongue and glass-like eyes.

"I see it!" Roy called out. The monster ran up the incline, its great claws digging into the mountain surface.

"It's out of the kill zone!" Roy called.

Ice-cold tingles ran up Felix's spine. Felix hadn't known Roy long, but knew him well enough to predict what the man was about to do.

Roy stepped sideways and leveled his shotgun. The Gorgon sprinted past Roy.

BANG BANG

Slugs tore into the monster's side. Slamming his finger into the trigger well of the under-barrel flame thrower attachment, Roy let loose a blanket of flame.

The Gorgon howled in a high tenor that held the power of a tuba. In its confused, agonized state, the monster sprinted, circling Roy. Roy—fearing the risk of fratricide—refused to shoot another time. The monster sprung with its saber teeth. It grabbed hold of Roy.

"No!!!" Felix screamed and sprinted to his aid.

But it was too late. The monster, still in pain, fell to its side. The physics of the monster's mass and speed threw him into a rolling motion. Roy was caught by his chest.

The two rolled down the mountain.

"Roy!" Felix cried out.

But while Roy's death was inevitable, the man wasn't dead yet. He drew his TTI JW4 Pit Viper pistol from its holster. He jammed the hand cannon into the Gorgon's skull.

BANG

As the Gorgon continued its death roll—and as Roy fell to his death—he kept firing. Five more times, the shots rang out. Smoke rose from the Gorgon's head. They rolled toward the vertical wall of the canyon.

Free of the mountain, the two went airborne—crashing toward the ground.

WHAAM

The two slammed into the creek bed. Rocks flew out from their impact. They sunk into the silt beneath the sediment-covered soil.

A rush of adrenaline fueled Felix. The BIA agent stowed his shotgun, then sprinted to the rope. He yanked on his gloves and descended. He rappelled down with one hand behind and the other guiding the rope above. He made it down in four controlled leaps against the vertical canyon wall.

"Roy!" Felix cried out. "Roy!"

Felix shot his legs out like a sprinter—long, explosive strides—with relaxed hands, he beat the air. Lactic acid tore into his quadriceps, but Felix, feeling the pain, only sprinted faster. His chest and lungs heaved in pain as his tactical vest clung to his body. The dry, desert heat amplified the full-body misery. He wiped bits of limestone from his eyes as he knelt beside Roy Raul.

"Buddy," Felix said. "You alright?"

Felix ripped his glove from his hand and placed it under Roy's chin, searching for a pulse. But despite his efforts, Felix's eyes told him the truth. Roy's mouth was frozen in an act of defiance. He bared his teeth in a wide smile with closed eyes. Blood ran from his mouth and nostrils from the sudden impact.

Felix stood back and observed the whole scene. The Gorgon lay dead. Smoke rose from its mouth and body. Blood no longer poured from its body; a static lake of scarlet liquid painted the sandy soil.

"Roy real did a number on that thing," Felix's facial muscles quivered as he observed Roy's death. "I'd say he bought the farm."

In Roy's dead hand, he still clutched a smoking Pit Viper pistol against the monster. While silt, blood, and bits of the beast sprinkled Roy's corpse, 1824 remained untouched.

"That dang *Tejano* killed that monster twice," Felix said, his voice cracking. "And once after he was pretty much dead."

Felix rose. The joints in his knees and lower back creaked. He stood in admiration of Roy's sacrifice. While the muscles in his face remained tight, giving him a mountain-like visage, tears flowed down his weary face.

"Felix!" a voice yelled behind him.

He turned to see Ben Andrade with his hands on his knees, panting from a sprint.

"Roy killed it," Felix sighed.

"Is he...?" Ben started. "Did...?"

"Don't ask me," Felix shook his head. "Look for yourself, but don't ask me again."

"Then he's not the only one."

"What do you mean?" Felix asked.

Ben stood up, continuing to breathe with heavy gasps. "When they fell. It created a rockslide. I got out of the way, but..."

"Jimbo didn't?"

Ben nodded. "A boulder smashed him in the head. It crushed his skull. Jimbo is dead."

CHAPTER 29

Felix American Pony

"Mission accomplished," Felix sighed, staring at the dead Gorgon. The monster's carcass pinned the dead Roy Raul against the Big Bend State Park desert floor.

"Hey," Ben patted Felix on the shoulder with a heavy hand, "you can't blame yourself."

Felix avoided Ben's gaze, then found his face growing into an involuntary sneer.

"What?" Felix asked. He shivered as he saw the two snake bites on the man's hand. He felt Ben's sweat-soaked hand still hanging onto his shoulder. Felix turned his head, almost as if Ben had to remind himself of the somberness of the situation and cast his eyes downward.

"Take me to see him," Felix's voice grew weaker. "I gotta see Jimbo."

"It isn't pretty," Ben's voice remained monotone, forcing Felix's skin into goosebumps.

"Felix," a voice from above said.

Looking up, Felix saw his friend, Japanese SDF Soldier Duke Hattori, scaling the rope. Duke sprinted to his side.

"It's dead," Felix said.

"Yeah," Duke panted. "I can see that. I do have a question though, about the monster."

Felix said nothing but looked at his friend.

"The way it ran," Duke said. "It wasn't hunting."

"Yeah," Felix said, "I picked up on that too."

"What do you mean?" Ben asked.

"It looked like it was in some sort of mad rage," Duke said.

Felix nodded.

"Mad rage?" Ben laughed. "What does that even mean?"

"It means," Duke said, "it acted weird."

"Weird, how?"

Felix stared at the twin pricks on the man's hand, "I don't know. You're the amateur reptile handler, you tell me."

"I think we can't answer that," Ben said. "Technically, I don't know if we can call it a reptile. It's a synapsid."

Felix's facial muscles twitched. *Why is one of the most intelligent men I know playing dumb?*

"Well, that creature was definitely acting weird," Felix said. "I'm with Duke on this one."

"Looked like it was just run—"

"But," Ben pointed in the air, emphasizing his point, "that replicant has been under the cartel's leash. Now, it's free."

Felix stiffened at the treasurer's interruption.

"I've seen people with no docs sprint," Felix said. "And I've seen victims *flee.*"

"I think what you're saying," Ben tapped his finger to his lip, "is that this... monster... was running away like an abused spouse."

A rush of hot heat ran through Felix's body. With clenched fists, he stepped forward. Duke stepped forward, trying to assuage his friend. As he did, Ben set his hand on Felix's shoulder.

"I spoke ignorantly," Ben said. "It sounds as though you have a heart for battered women."

Felix slapped Ben's hand off his shoulder, then, with both hands, shoved Ben. The treasurer flew backward. His feet washed in the air as he arched upward and slammed into the ground.

I'd call that pancake, Felix thought, his mind rushing back to his football career.

Ben moaned, then rolled to his side. He sat up, his sweat-soaked hair in disarray and his face confused by what had just happened. *But it doesn't look like he ever played.*

"That's assault!" Ben said, his voice cracking. "You're a federal officer and you just assaulted me."

"You put your hand on my shoulder," Felix said. "I felt threatened."

"Are you crazy?" Ben asked.

"You remind me of a toxic salesman," Felix stepped forward, his boots almost touching Ben's. "Trying to convince me my whole life has been wasted 'til I'm buying something from them."

"What are you talking about?" Ben's voice cracked high.

"What are you trying to sell?" Felix said, watching the treasurer rise to his feet.

Ben dusted off his knees and looked at his hands. Felix watched as Ben winced and pulled burs from his hand.

"Did you play football or something?" Ben asked. "That was quite a hit."

"You ain't seen nothin' yet."

"Look," Ben said. "I think I struck a nerve."

"You're trying to make me second guess myself," Felix said. "I might not be as smart as you, but I can feel it. Something was wrong with that creature."

"*Feel* it..." Ben shook his head as if to apologize for his interruption.

"That thing," Duke interrupted. "to put it in slang terms, 'ran willy nilly.' Not like a skilled predator."

"Duke's right," Felix said. "It's kinda like..."

"Like," Duke Hattori said, casting his eyes from Ben to Felix, "it was running *from* something."

CHAPTER 30

Tennyson

"Tell me," Tennyson said, "what are we up against?"

He stood with the cartel aviator in the destroyed airplane. Bits of glass, debris, pieces of limestone, and cactus covered the area. The leather clad, long-haired man who flew the plane for the cartels was pinned to his seat, immobilized by the severity of his injuries.

"I don't reach out to Feds," the dying man said.

Tennyson, despite his own pain, laughed. He had spent the entirety of his adult life in a THC stupor, so to be mistaken for a cop humored him.

"You look like you used to buy our product," the man said. "I don't give out secrets."

"What is El Mee-mow? How is there a dinosaur running around Big Bend?"

"It's now my turn to laugh," he said.

And as the smuggler laughed, Tennyson turned away, avoiding the sight of the man coughing up blood in his mirth.

"They were *de mi capo*."

"*Capo*? You mean, like your... godfather?"

The man laughed again; more blood spilled from his mouth.

"Write this down." Reaching toward his leg, he handed Tennyson a weathered notebook with a pencil attached by string.

Tennyson nodded and took the paper and pen.

"*Mi Familia* never brought violence to Americans or *su gente*. We don't normally talk to authorities but you have to write that down. *El Mimo* and his...*discípulos* shot us down. They got loose."

"El Mee-mow and his...?"

"His gang, but it's hard to explain. They follow him. But they don't act like a gang... it's just violence."

Tennyson, despite his overwhelming physical agony, fought the urge to laugh. The cartel aviator had probably been connected to hundreds of murders, but in the gangster's mind those were justified by the pursuit of profit.

"They just do things."

He waved Tennyson closer and took the writing utensils. The aviator wrote on the pad and handed it back.

"'El Mimo,'" Tennyson read. "'It means the mime.'"

"*Buen*—good, now write more. He and his crew. He shot us down...for a reason *no puedo* understand. *El Mimo* let them loose."

Tennyson scribbled on the pad with frantic fingers. He stopped, inspecting what he had written. A kaleidoscope of butterflies flew through Tennyson's stomach. It could have been due to the aviator's agony, but he was losing his command of the English language. Still, despite his unkempt appearance, the man gave an impression of professional knowledge. He knew the man hadn't been confused in his dictation.

Tennyson circled the word:

Them.

"You're saying that the monster I saw isn't alone? You're telling me there's more than one?"

CHAPTER 31

Felix American Pony

Felix breathed with yoga-style inhales as he stood at the bottom of Fresno Canyon. Ben did possess multiple talents, but the man always had to be right. Ben had law enforcement experience and was a contractor, though he never served in the military. But his lack of training hadn't stopped him from putting his input into the tactical decisions. Even though Ben apologized, he couldn't change his characteristics or personality.

Ben Andrade isn't confident, Felix thought. *He's arrogant.*

Some of the most arrogant men Felix had met had been in law enforcement. But this felt different, even more exaggerated.

"From what Brody had told us," Felix started, "the bull was running erratically too. It was running from the Gorgon that hit Jorge's truck."

"Correct," Duke said, nodding.

"But," Ben interjected, "that would mean there are more. I know that wasn't in the intelligence brief...."

"So?" Felix shrugged. "Guys on the ground dictate intel, not the other way around. We'll send it to our intel guy and he can do his thing with it."

"I don't think that's a good idea," Ben said.

Felix started to step forward.

"Felix!" Duke Hattori yelled and grabbed Felix's shoulder.

He turned his head. Duke pointed up the mountain. "Radames is yelling at us. Something is coming!"

From the corner of his eye, Felix saw rapid movement. His eyes caught a blur.

Ben? Felix thought.

Ben ran away from the pair. Back to Jimmy Martinez' covered ambush position, thirty feet away.

Ben Andrade smiled. In his hand, he held up an Army green square object.

"That's the claymore!" Felix yelled and then tackled Duke. The pair slammed to the ground next to the Gorgon's corpse.

BOOM!

The claymore mine exploded. Projectiles mixed with limestone shot downward. Large broken slabs from the canyon's wall collapsed, burying Felix and Duke.

CHAPTER 32

Felix American Pony

"Duke," Felix whispered under all the debris, "you alive?"

Duke remained silent. Felix's stomach panted, waiting for his friend's reply.

"Duke!"

"For the second time!" Duke said, his voice strained to a hoarse whisper. "I said yes!"

"Oh," Felix laughed, realizing the blast had affected his hearing.

The explosion in Fresno Canyon had left them covered in detritus. When Felix realized Ben's intent to kill them with the claymore mine, he tackled Duke to the ground, shielding the JDF soldier from the blast. Once on the ground, Duke Hattori yanked the pair under the corpse as best he could. The creature, with the previous debris covering and its pachyderm-like flesh, shielded them.

"Ben betrayed us," Felix whispered. "He initiated the claymore."

Duke squirmed under the BIA agent, "What?"

"He tried to kill us."

"That makes no sense," Duke said. "That's like trying to kill an exterminator."

Felix noticed Duke's words grew softer as he spoke from the lack of oxygen.

"I can't see him," Felix wiggled back and forth, easing out of the corpse's shelter. He then dug through his vest and found his pair of hearing protection. Their form was identical to hearing aids. He stuffed them into his ears. The device amplified the sounds.

"I think I hear him," Felix whispered.

Something impacted the rocks outside; instead of multiple steps, the stones slid together.

"He's gotta be hurt," Felix whispered. "Sounds like he's dragging his leg."

The grind of sediment sliding against the soil continued. Felix furrowed his brow as he tried to understand the sound.

"I don't know if that's him."

"We need to get to Radames."

Felix edged further out. Shaking his head, he let bits of the limestone fall from him. Now free from the debris' hold, he could see. With careful precision, he twisted his head, scanning the area. Felix fought the urge to cough as the dust tickled his throat.

"I don't see the traitor," Felix said.

Felix pushed further out from the demolished area.

"What do you see?" Duke asked.

"I see…" Felix pushed even further out. "I see…"

Felix's whole body trembled. He fell back down as his knees and hands gave way. The silt slid back on him.

"You're acting weird," Duke said.

Felix opened his mouth, but as he trembled, his lips and tongue produced only stutters.

"What's up, Felix? You're scaring me."

Felix nodded, controlling his breathing.

"G-g-good," Felix managed.

"Felix!" Duke whispered. "What is it?"

Felix opened his mouth, but his words failed him. Felix American Pony, the man who set the ambush against the Gorgon and bravely patrolled the Sonoran Desert, shook with fear.

But while fear shook him, it couldn't stop him. Felix closed his eyes and began Vinyasa-style breathing, calming his system.

"I know," Felix said. "I know why the Gorgon was running."

CHAPTER 33

Felix American Pony

With careful precision, the two men pushed away from the Gorgon. Broken slabs from the Fresno Canyon fell as they struggled to stand.

"Get your weapon ready," Felix whispered.

"You'll need to switch to your pistol," Duke said.

Felix looked down. Dirt caked his long arm.

"Same thing happened to mine," Duke said.

Felix cursed. Pulling on the sling, he pushed the shotgun to his back and drew his pistol. Both men assumed a good low ready position and walked forward.

Felix kept his right hand on the pistol and pointed with his left, "There."

Felix kept his eyes forward, weapon drawn, and his whole body shook with terror. He heard Duke speaking in Japanese.

"You have to point," Duke whispered. "I see it."

A giant, legless, scale-covered monster lay before them, stretched across the canyon's floor.

The great snake had black coils, thick and diamond-shaped, that formed impenetrable shields. Felix shuddered as its muscles flexed to propel forward. With ease, it slithered in a horrible S-shaped pattern.

"Martinez!" Duke yelled. "It's trying to eat him."

Duke opened fire. Still concerned about his foreground and backdrop, Felix angled away from the monster's head to not hit Martinez and slammed his finger into the trigger well.

With terrifying grace, the great snake swung its head toward them. Its head reached over ten feet in the air. It hissed and bared its fangs.

BANG BANG BANG

Both men shot at the abomination. It hissed louder as the rounds impacted. It weaved its head left to right, avoiding the blast. The monster shot its head forward.

BOOM

BOOM

A shotgun slug tore into the beast. It shrieked in pain.

"RADAMES!" Duke shouted and pointed above.

The Mexican soldier fired his FX-05 Xiuhcoat. The snake ripped its head away and darted, leaving a trail of dust shooting skyward. A cacophony, similar to rockslides, sounded as the colossal creature slithered away.

CHAPTER 34

Felix American Pony

Felix winced as he saw blood dripping from the back of Duke's head and onto the Fresno Canyon soil.

"Duke," Felix said, "you're bleeding."

"How bad?" Duke asked. His jet hair was knotted with blood. As Duke asked, Radames finished descending the rope and sprinted to their position.

"Let me put something on that," Felix said, pointing Radames to Jimbo's rucksack.

Radames knew Felix was referring to Jimbo's medical kit. The Mexican soldier ran to the ruck, dug through it, and sprinted back.

"Here," Radames said. In the soldier's face, Felix saw that the man had something to say. But Felix couldn't speak right now. Taking the Israeli bandage, he put it on the wound and tightened it down. Felix manipulated it so Duke could still see.

"We'll need to change that out every few hours," Felix said.

"Agh," Duke said. "We got hundred-mile-an-hour tape."

"*El Serpiento!*" Radames panted.

"Which one?" Felix asked Radames while working on the bandage.

"*¿Que?*" Radames asked.

"Ben Andrade," Felix hissed. "He turned turncoat. He ambushed us."

"Ben?" Radames asked, gaping as he did.

"He set the claymore off," Felix finished Duke's wrap and turned to face Radames.

"Through the chaos," Radames said. "I now understand his course-of-action."

"You mean that Ben's a traitor?"

Radames shook his head, "Jimbo's hydration kit. It was torn up. I wasn't able to further investigate, but I believe it was slashed with a knife. The ruck is soaking wet, but the camelback is dry."

"You're saying we're dry?" Duke touched his head.

"No matter," Felix said with a grim determination. "We've got the chlorine tablets—"

"These were also stored in Jimbo's rucksack," Radames stated calmly. "However, they are currently missing."

"Ben Andrade," Felix hissed. "He must've been planning this all along. Probably paid off by the cartel."

Radames shook his head, "Not likely. Cartels typically adhere to a set of guidelines, and acts of violence against Americans are not a common occurrence in this region."

"And I vouched for him," Felix said. "I ran his background check and personally administered his polygraph."

Felix cursed and punched his own thigh.

Small details rushed into his mind. Ben was arrogant. Ben didn't mind touching dead things; he might have even enjoyed it. Ben excelled at the polygraph. And if Ben didn't get paid by the cartels, he did this for enjoyment.

Ben was a psychopath.

Felix sighed. Ben might be a sociopath, or it might just mean Felix wasn't a psychologist. He couldn't assign a label.

"Guys," Duke said. "We gotta get out of this kill zone. Especially if Ben is out there."

Felix nodded and pointed at Jimbo's rucksack. "Salvage what we can. Destroy the rest."

"Ben!" Duke spat as he dug through Jimbo's ruck. "He's already torn through it."

Felix's whole body grew weak. His knees trembled and bile crept into his throat.

This is my fault. I let Ben out here.

"Ben killed Jimbo," Felix said.

Jimbo's rucksack—which had once been robust, with equipment pushing against the ALICE frame—was now almost empty, leaving only toiletries and clothes.

"He has also betrayed us," Radames stated with resignation. "We have nothing left."

"Ben took Jimbo's sapper supplies, dried out the water!" Duke added. "How can we do it? We have to stop Ben! We have to kill the snake!"

Felix cast his eyes back over at the dead Gorgon.

"We said that it was thirty feet long, right?"

The other two soldiers looked at the debris-covered beast.

"*Pero*, that isn't nine meters," Radames said.

"No," Felix spat, "it ain't."

"You mean...?" Duke asked.

"The first one," Felix nodded, "is still out there."

"We gotta get out of here," Duke shook his head. "But, where?"

"*Necessitamos* eliminate the threat," Radames said.

"Yeah," Duke laughed, "but which one? And how?"

Felix looked over the Fresno Canyon floor. The cruel desert heat tore into him as he thought. The once beautiful scene of the sheer limestone walls and desert orations of cactus and other fauna now presented as a dangerous obstacle. If the traitor or the replicants didn't kill them, Big Bend still could.

"We're stuck out in the desert with no water. No resources." Felix, the lone surviving American in the group, scratched his chin. "Looks like we're shootin' from the hip."

CHAPTER 35

Felix American Pony

"As Franklin Pierce once said," Felix pointed north toward the direction of the Fresno Cascades, "only thing left to do is drink."

They had to slay dragons, but first, they had to make it to water.

Actually, Franklin Pierce said the only thing left is to get drunk, Felix thought. But he didn't want to air American dirty laundry in front of foreigners.

The Chihuahuan Desert's lethality was matched only by its strange beauty. Mesquite bushes with parakeet-shaded leaves extended from gnarled, tilted branches along the sandy desert floor. Crowned atop the emerald, spine-covered cacti were purple-cheeked pitayas. Whip-tailed lizards sprinted in the sand as a committee of turkey vultures glided in an annular pattern, wafting in the rising scent of ichor.

"I feel like Ben had some plan," Felix said as they approached the Cascades, "but my mind doesn't understand."

"Tengo miedo que I can't answer," Radames licked his lips, his eyes never leaving the water ahead. "I think this could potentially lead to war between Mexico and the US."

"Can I tell you something potentially offensive?" Duke asked.

Felix and Radames looked at one another and then back at their friend.

"What's up?" Felix asked.

"And you promise you won't laugh?" Duke asked.

"No," Felix chortled through cracked lips, "I need a laugh."

Duke sighed, "When I was a teenager, I was..."

Duke stopped talking and adjusted his vest. He gave a sidelong look at Radames, and his face reddened.

"I... was in the Japanese subculture that wore cholo-style clothing."

"Wait... wait," Felix laughed, "Captain Duke Hattori wore the flannel shirt—"

"Black bandana over my shaved head, white shirt, Dickies," Duke started with his eyes cast downward. Despite his embarrassment, a renewed passion sounded in his voice, "Black, beautifully crafted, black-stitched Converse tennis shoes, and completing my look was a gold chain with a pendant with an Aztec skull with a headdress."

"Cultural nuances can be misinterpreted," Radames said. "*Pero,* that's American culture, I think Felix should be the one to be offended."

"I'm not from Los Angeles," Felix coughed from his dehydrated laughter.

"I just mean to say," Duke continued, "that my heart is hurting. Growing up in Japan, I was fascinated with that culture. Those two countries that inspired me so much may go to war. My heart is broken for my friends and the strings tear for the future."

Felix's stomach flipped as he listened to the conversation.

"Passion will outpour from the hearts of Americans enraged from the cartels' bloodshed on their soil. But use your heart," the JDF soldier responded. "Think about the cruelty in the first kill. The victim was torn apart. Even Jorge's donkey. Mistreating animals will get people riled up too. If it is believed cartels are responsible, Americans will unite against not just the individual cartel responsible but cartels as a whole and any entity attached."

Felix rubbed his left shoulder with his right hand, "You guys got my stomach tied in knots. You feel like replicants could lead to a war?"

"Easily," Duke said.

Radames stroked his chin, "I find Duke's reasoning—though guided more by passion than I normally feel comfortable with—aligns with logic."

"My heart is ripped apart by what happened to our friends. My mind is too tired to reason," Felix said, "but my gut tells me something is wrong. I just can't quite put my finger on it."

Radames snapped his finger, "That's it."

Felix felt himself drawing his pistol, assuming an excellent extended position. "What? Where?"'

"Lo siento," Radames said. "No, not a security issue. I was thinking, Duke is right."

Felix gritted his teeth and slammed his pistol back into its holster.

"No," Radames continued, "analytically, primordial creatures being released in Big Bend State Park doesn't immediately make you think of a war, but the heart..."

Duke nodded and patted his chest with a closed fist.

"The heart cries out for justice, dare I say even revenge!" Duke said.

"Pero," Radames added, "where does Ben fall in all of this?"

The trio stopped at the water. Felix drew his pistol, allowing the other two men to drink water and refill their hydration kits. There was a high risk of sickness, but dirty water was better than dehydration.

"Your mind's gonna be demanding the answer to that question," Felix said. "Your brains might be telling you one thing, but let's not ignore that gut feeling. Right now, we're piecing it together, but something tells me Ben's in the mix. Somehow, someway, he's behind this mess."

CHAPTER 36

The Gorgon

Felix's analysis had been correct.

The great Gorgon still prowled Big Bend. After resting, the monster's meals cleared his stomach, allowing him unfettered movement. The monster coated its whiskers with saliva by tracing them with its rough, black tongue. Like a cello-bow caked in resin, the whiskers now rang clearer. Sounds and smells ran to the monster.

Its eyes glazed in almost sensual ecstasy: it smelled humans. The sweet, iron smell of spilled blood floated skyward. Its eyes burst with excitement. It sprinted with a terrible grace down from El Solitario. Its blood-laced paws balanced it along the strange geology of the Texan volcano. With ease, it reached the level surface and continued its sprint. With no decline, its speed increased. The earth zoomed past the Gorgon as it sprinted. It kept its mouth open, allowing the air to creep in.

In its own animalistic way, the monster felt freedom and joy as the air skittered across its scales, cooling off its body in the intense Texas heat. Its whole body grew warm; goosebump-like sensations chilled its body as it smelled the blood.

The ichor scent brought him to Fresno Canyon. With a bestial sense of merriment, the creature bounded into the dried creek bed.

Something was different.

Not only did his sense alert him to the smell of human carcasses. Another scent wafted into its nostrils, sending a strange message into its brain. Its tail whipped left to right in an anxiety-like emotion as it followed the trail.

The monster first saw Jimbo's body. With involuntary and immediate fervor, its mouth salivated. Despite its sudden carnal urge, curiosity drove it forward and away from the fallen fighter.

What was this strange new scent?

The monster saw Roy Raul's body. Animals could smell fear in a person, but Roy was the opposite. The monster could sense the bravery and defiance that covered the fighter in a particular scent.

In its original settings—the cartel's laboratory and then the drug lord's land—it hadn't been able to hunt. Its master had thrown bounded victims into its realm, and now, the monster's empire had expanded. Blood lust and the thrill of the hunt now consumed it. New sensations shook the beast. Yes, passion, the excitement to feed and devour the downed bodies. Something different struck the beast.

Then he saw it:

The body of the fallen smaller Gorgon.

It pushed its snout forward, allowing it to tap the carcass of its kind. The smaller Gorgon had been matched for a particular purpose for the larger:

It had been designed to be its mate.

Its whole body shook.

The Gorgon was a replicant designed to mirror the form of the Gorgon Synapsid. Its structure, though almost identical save for its exaggerated size, had resulted from cellular manipulation while it was an embryo. Scientists reverse-engineered and manipulated its cellular system, creating its monstrous form.

In the creation of the monster, it had been determined that it needed a mate.

But the scientists hadn't given it a mate to produce offspring. The female was designed because of the monster's need for companionship. It needed a female to prevent sexual frustration. The Gorgon had many feline characteristics, and a thirty-foot primordial tomcat, unable to release its seed, would be a menace to anything near it.

The Gorgon sat a paw on the female monster's carcass. Science had warned about anthropomorphizing fauna, but the animal kingdom's emotional complexity was too challenging to describe. As Jane Goodall had shown the world in her research, describing animals in human terms was the only way to adequately communicate with the outside world. Despite this monster's lust for human flesh and aggressiveness toward all living things, it still had specific reactions. Scientists would refuse to attribute emotions like fear and remorse to an animal, but the Gorgon's emotional state could be easily seen:

The monster was sad.

It no longer had the opportunity for companionship or the ability to release its seed. Its female companion was dead. The humans had placed a curse on its existence, sentencing it to isolation. It rubbed its snout with tender touch against the female's bloody skull.

It was alone.

Now, the only one of its kind, it would be forever alone.

And as it soothed its heartache, another strange scent shook it. From the female's head, it walked toward her lower body. Debris from the failed ambush covered her. It smacked at the detritus using its powerful paws, clearing it from its fallen mate. It crept forward and placed its head over her hindquarters.

It fell back on its haunches and tilted its head skyward. It released a mournful howl, a cry that combined pity and horror. The female hadn't died alone. A specific odor wafted from her loins.

She had been with child.

CHAPTER 37

Felix American Pony

Felix looked through his binoculars as his two desperate friends drank water from the Fresno Cascades.

What is that?

A trail of dust shot high into the air. His mind rushed to the snake. As his mind ran to that legless fiend, other portions of his body, all connected to his mind, did too. He could remember the smells and sensations he encountered when he first saw the beast at Fresno Canyon.

"Guys, get ready," Felix said. "It's coming back!"

"We have nada," he heard Radames whisper.

Felix's whole body tightened as, through the binos, he saw the trail of dust approaching. The Gorgon had terrified Felix, but this serpent created a different sense of terror with its spear-shaped head, forked tongue, and scales. Its limbless motion seemed so alien as it swam over the desert soil. The engineers must have had a particularly sick sense of humor when they gave the monster its black color with red scales striping its eyes.

Felix shuddered.

Where can we hide?

The monster had skittered away through the harsh Chihuahuan Desert, immune to the terrible Texas terrain. Not only did the environment seem unable to prevent its forward movement, but the eldritch rhythm of its locomotion would cause them all to pause.

As Felix watched the dust draw nearer, his whole body shook. Like rats, they had crammed themselves into a crevasse of the mountain. Pistols had little to no effect and the great serpent had seemed to shrug off Radames' rifle rounds as well. But if all rounds concentrated on its head, the results would have been different. Felix remained outside, pulling security.

That doesn't look like a snake, he thought. He pulled his head back from the binos and tried to understand the situation.

"That looks like a… tank," Felix said aloud.

Felix recognized the vehicle.

"That's a RIPSAW F4."

It was a tank that could travel up to fifty miles an hour. It had a cab similar to a truck. While the chassis couldn't support the weight of a traditional tank's main gun, it still provided excellent cover for terrain like this.

The Ripsaw stopped, kicking up rocks as the heavy-duty rubber tracks skidded to a stop.

"This might complicate things with Radames," Felix said. He had heard of Latin American military units defecting to the cartels and rumors of those units crossing international borders to sell illicit products.

"But, a tank?" Felix scratched his head. "And does any Central American army have a tank that highspeed?"

Using the binos, he traced his eyes all over the rolling weapon. On the tank, Felix spied a tattoo-like design, expertly drawn and placed on the cab.

"Does that tank have a killer clown tattoo?"

From his time in law enforcement, Felix had seen similar designs. But this one was different. It wasn't a traditional Euro-centric clown. The picture had a white face, like a clown, but was also made to look like a skull, like images seen on Dia De Muertos decorations. Atop the terrifying white painted face was a black beret.

"That's not a clown," Felix adjusted the lenses. "That's a mime."

Felix held up his radio to his lips and thumbed the mic to speak.

Suddenly, Ben Andrade stepped out from a hidden position. The traitor waved and walked toward the tank.

"Ben?"

Rage shook Felix. He wanted to kill the coward, but his pistols couldn't reach that distance and would only serve to alert the tank to his position.

"A picture worth a thousand words," Felix said. Setting his binos down, he grabbed his smartphone from his vest. Using a special camera application on his phone, he zoomed in and thumbed the button.

And as he did, a man stood up from the hatch.

"Is this guy serious?"

The man walked from the back of the tank and then to Ben. He wore what looked like black tactical overalls. Pistols, knives, a radio, and other assorted tactical tools adorned the overall's Bible. The man wore no visible shirt underneath, exposing thick, jet-colored chest hair, with wiry, vein-covered muscles. On his hands were black opera gloves that stretched to his elbows. His face was painted identical to the design: white face paint covered his face with black marks around his eyes and nose. Along his mouth was a thin line, with stitches to give it a more skull-like impression. Adorning his long, black, shoulder-length hair was a black beret.

"You guys need to see this," Felix whispered into his mic. "Stay low but come out here."

"Roger," Duke said into the radio.

Felix lay flat against the ground, still watching the pair.

"What you got, buddy?" Duke said, as he lay down beside Felix.

The BIA agent handed the Japanese self-defense soldier his binos.

"I see Ben... I see... a tank?" Duke's voice grew quieter, "and a guy in white face paint..."

"What did you just say?" Radames asked.

"Here," Duke handed the binos to Radames.

The Mexican soldier held the device to his eyes.

"¡*Chingada*!" Radames gritted his teeth.

Felix and Duke looked at one another and then back at Radames.

"We've located the stolen tank," Radames shook his head.

"That's a stolen tank?" Duke asked.

Radames cast his eyes downward, as if to hide his shame, "From the cartel."

"Cartels have tanks?"

"You guys have Yakuza—"

"Guys!" Felix interjected, calming the situation. "What's going on? With the tank? With the mime?"

Radames shook his head. While at *Heroico Colegio Militar* he had majored in mathematics. Reason and logic were how he operated but now—now he was shaken by emotions as shame ensnared him. A problem that he worked to solve in his home country had now spread north and others would know. He closed his eyes, focusing on the problem and the color rushed from his face, "The moniker is El Mimo. And he is the most dangerous part of this story."

CHAPTER 38

Felix American Pony

"What is an El Mimo?" Duke asked, whispering as they crouched behind the rocks of the Fresno Cascades of Big Bend.

"No, no, *who* is El Mimo?" Felix shook his head, then turned to Radames. "He stole a tank? From a cartel?"

"I would describe the man as insane," Radames still looked through the binos, "but I think my analysis falls short."

"And what is Ben doing with him?" Felix asked. "Ben's a conniver, but he ain't crazy."

"I do not believe El Mimo fits within that categorization either," Radames stated evenly, lowering the binoculars and passing them back to Felix.

"You just said he was insane," Felix said.

"I said I would *describe* him that way," Radames got to his knees, continuing to scout the area, "but that's only because I have no other way to rationally characterize such an individual. No medical term directly relates to El Mimo."

"He attacks the cartels?" Duke asked. "You should be thrilled."

"No," Radames shook his head, "he attacks everything. Anything that presents any sort of order."

Felix also moved to his knees and pulled his assault pack to his back.

"I feel like you're trying to say that El Mimo is an anarchist." Felix tightened the straps on his bag.

Radames pointed to the water, letting the others know where he wanted to go.

"Hmm..." Radames scratched his chin, *"pero* there were some political motivations."

"Political?" Felix twisted his body sideways as he walked down the slope.

"Are you familiar with the Zimmerman note?" Radames grunted as he descended.

"That's kind of an awkward question coming from you," Felix asked.

Radames looked left to right. "*Creo que,* at this time, it is best I disclose a history long recognized within the Mexican intelligence community."

"What are you trying to say?" Felix grunted as they continued their hike.

"The Germans' attempt at the instigation of war was not unique to the US-Mexican border."

"How so?"

Radames stopped walking and cast his eyes downward. He flexed his facial features as he struggled with his thought.

"Vichy France," Radames said.

"The French puppet state?" Felix asked.

Radames winced, "A little more complicated than that."

"What does El Mimo have to do with Vichy France?" Felix scratched his head.

"First, the cultural significance of the mime." Radames pointed in the air. "Then, Imperial Japan requested help neutralizing the Aztec Eagles, which had been so detrimental to their endeavors in the Pacific. Nazi Germany, in trying to keep strong relations with their Japanese counterpart, agreed and attempted to push Vichy France into war with Germany."

"That doesn't make any sense," Felix shook his head.

"Indeed, that is a plausible interpretation," Radames countered, his voice measured and analytical. "Mexico's defeat of the French military undoubtedly left a lasting impression. The Nazis likely perceived an opportunity in exploiting the desire for retribution and leveraging it to their advantage. Moreover, the prospect of expanding the conflict to North America would have significant strategic implications."

"So, is he an anarchist or a Vichy France supporter?" Felix said as the trio continued to walk down north through Big Bend State Park.

Radames scratched his chin, "It's ironic."

"Come on, Radames," Felix said, snapping with evident impatience. "We're not here for a debate. We need answers, not musings about philosophy."

The Mexican soldier held his hands up. "It's paradoxical. Some of the most violent protests are ones for peace. Similarly, to combat the threat of a communist government takeover, liberal democracy used government overreach."

"Get to the point," Felix rolled his eyes.

"I'm saying that El Mimo is both." Radames pointed in the area.

"An authoritarian and an anarchist?" Felix felt his body grow hot, angered by his own confusion.

"In World War II, certain Nazi factions attempted to persuade Vichy France to attempt to recapture Mexico and avenge themselves from Cinco de Mayo," Radames said. "French monarchists who supported Philippe Pétain still possessed intense animosity with the US because of the Federalist support of the Haitian Revolution. Alexander Hamilton's assistance with the Haitian Constitution further strained Franco-American relations and Vichy France had not forgotten. The French Fascist Government dispatched commando units to gather intelligence in Mexico. However, before their plans could materialize, the defeat of Hitler by the Allies altered the course of events. The Vichy France intelligence gatherers, unable to return home, remained. Just as hundreds of thousands of Germans and Nazis fled to Argentina, so some descendants of Vichy France commandos remained in *mi casa*."

"I feel where this is going," Felix said. "He's not a traditional anarchist, but seeing the failure of French colonialism, he grew angry—"

"Yes," Radames nodded with signature stoicism. "If his master Philippe Pétain lacked control, chaos would be the only alternative he would accept."

"That's it!" Felix said. "El Mimo somehow must have let the cartel's replicants loose in order to instigate war between our two great resources."

"But my question," Radames started, "is why did Ben Andrade join El Mimo? How did El Mimo know about the replicants?"

"You're thinking it just in terms of numbers and rational thought," Duke said, countering Radames. "For Ben, it's an easy answer. Ben was mean and was attracted to anything that would let him be that way. Murderers and thugs traveled to Syria to join ISIS. Unlike other terrorist organizations, ISIS recruits just joined to kill."

"And his intelligence of the genetic engineering?" Felix asked. "Who let a psycho like El Mimo know about that?"

"As far as El Mimo's knowledge of the replicants, that's easy. Many Axis scientists fled prosecution or were given positions of power. His network would have shared that information."

"This will result in war," Radames said.

"We can't let this happen," Duke said. "My heart says we find El Mimo and put down the threat."

"Listen up," Felix said. "If we stop him—if we can kill El Mimo—it'll free up Mondragon and the others to kill the monsters."

"*Pero*, our situation is devoid of resources," Radames countered.

"You heard me, *amigo*," Felix pointed north, "we'll make it up as we go."

Radames laughed and shook his head, "*Gringos*."

CHAPTER 39

Felix American Pony

Felix held up a Big Bend State Park map as the trio walked north.

"Here!" He pointed to the paper while still moving. "This is where we are headed."

Radames took the map, "Torres' Exotics."

"Exotics?" Duke asked. "As in exotic animals?"

"Yup," Felix nodded as they continued north.

"I don't know about you guys," Duke laughed, "but I think I'm done seeing exotics."

"I agree with you," Radames said.

"I am there with you guys, trust me," Felix said. "But we can't afford not to venture there. We have no resources. And that place will have some I'm looking for."

"As in using the animals for bait?" Radames scratched his head. "I thought we were focused on El Mimo?"

"C'mon, Radames," Felix chided. "You're the one with the big brain. What resources would a farm have?"

Radames snapped his fingers, "Got you."

"What are you guys talking about?" Duke asked.

"He's saying that a farm will have feed. It'll probably have hay," Radames answered.

"And," Duke's eyes lit up, "hay will need fertilizer…"

"And if we have fertilizer," Radames said, "we have a bomb."

CHAPTER 40

Yennifer Santa-Anna

"Mi sancha," Oliver Olivera said as he reached to kiss Yennifer Santa-Anna.

"I told you not to call me that," Yennifer snapped her head sideways. Her bleached blonde hair slapped him in the face.

"Oh, c'mon, baby," Oliver said.

"Are we even supposed to be here?" she asked. "This looks like it's off limits."

"I told you," he said, "its Tapado Canyon. It's a hike to get here, but it's worth it."

"Would you take your wife here?" She slammed her hand against the desert floor, "Or would you have taken her out in a more public place?"

"Yennifer—"

"I never wanted to be your mistress. You said you'd marry me!"

Oliver sighed; he stood up and started to walk toward their tent.

"No!" she yelled. "You can sleep outside!"

"But—"

"If that's the only thing you use me for," she laughed, "then it looks like it's the only thing I can control."

"But I burned through my sick leave to be with you."

Yennifer, still sitting on the ground, turned away from Oliver. She heard him curse under his breath and tear at the tent's zipper. She felt him stomp against the ground as he marched past her.

Yennifer, remaining silent, entered the tent. She zipped the door. She removed her makeup, and remaining fully clothed, kicked her legs into her sleeping bag. After such a tiring day, it didn't take long to fall asleep.

Not long after, Yennifer woke as the tent shook.

A voice called out: "Baby, baby!"

"I'm not talking to you, Oliver!"

"It's not what you think," his voice trembled. *"Ayúdame,* please."

"Oliver?" her voice squeaked as her mind fought to understand the situation.

"Por favor Sancha, por favor," he whispered.

"I told you..." she trailed off as she heard what she assumed was Oliver trembling. "Oliver?"

His breath grew quieter.

"It's not funny, Oliver!"

But despite her frustration, Yennifer's heart stung. She crept to her knees and slid open the door with slow, careful fingers. No industrial light pollution affected the night sky in Presidio County. While this allowed for great star-gazing, it also decreased almost all illumination. Yennifer shook with fear as she stared into the night, which only bits of lunar rays illuminated.

"Oliver," she whispered. "Oliver!"

A mesquite bush shook as Oliver stood up. While Big Bend had vegetation, it didn't provide cover. Spines and pricks covered the flora, which left Yennifer puzzled when she saw Oliver standing beside a mesquite tree.

"You okay?" she winced as she thought of the rough that would be slicing into Oliver's skin.

Oliver shook his head and stepped forward.

Yennifer gulped; her eyes bulged.

Oliver's pants were stained, and he had soiled his pants.

"Honey?"

He raised his arms in a child-like manner and tottered forward. Yennifer rushed toward him. He wrapped her in his arms, pressing her body against his. She fought against the bile that spewed up her throat as the aroma of excrement stung her senses. She moved out of the hug but still clutched his hand.

"Let's g-g-go," he said.

"Did you see a bear or something?"

Oliver stared at her with pitiful bulging eyes. He nodded.

"Atras," he said, "let's go back to the truck."

Yennifer reached back toward the tent. Oliver yanked her hand. A sharp, overwhelming pain hit her collarbone.

"You're hurting me!" she grunted. "We can go, fine, let's go."

The pair started their long hike south. Multiple emotions hit Yennifer, and while she struggled to cope, she still believed hiking south was the answer.

"Uh-uh-uh-uh," Oliver's lips shook. With adrenaline-filled strength, he gripped Yennifer's hand. She brought her other hand to his, trying to break his grip. She looked down, but when the grip loosened, she breathed a sigh of relief.

"Oli—"

Then she saw it.

The great Gorgon prowled behind them. Despite its massive size—a thirty-foot body—the monster stepped forward in silence.

"Here!" Oliver said. Yennifer felt two hands slam into her back, shoving her forward. Her chest hit the rocky ground. Her collarbone—

already bruised—smacked into a big, gray rock. She screamed as her collarbone snapped. The bone penetrated her flesh, exposing the white bone from the collar. The side of her head slammed against the hot sandy floor.

Despite her pain, she could hear Oliver behind her. She heard him hobbling away from her in a shambling gait.

But while Oliver ran behind her, the beast was before her.

"No!" she screamed and closed her eyes as the Gorgon sprinted at her. She felt the beast's massive weight slam into her knee. She cried out in pain as she felt her leg buckle backward.

But then the Gorgon left her. It sprinted over her and past her.

Straight toward Oliver.

"Ayúdame!" he cried as the Gorgon pounced. The monster's front limbs landed on the man's torso, slamming him to the ground. They both hit the ground so hard that rocks and dust shot outward from their impact. Yennifer watched as the monster shot its head forward. It bit into Oliver's head and then released.

Oliver screamed. As the monster bit and slapped Oliver with its paws, Yennifer understood what was happening. Though covered in rough pachyderm-like skin, the Gorgon had strong feline characteristics. She shuddered as she watched the Gorgon bite Oliver's leg and toss him skyward.

As the screaming Oliver went airborne, the monster jumped up and caught the man in its mouth. Yennifer had seen house cats demonstrate similar behavior when they caught a mouse; cats would leave the rat alive and practice their hunting skills. Oliver screamed as the Gorgon slammed both paws into Oliver's legs. She knew what it was doing. It was playing with Oliver; it was playing with its prey.

CHAPTER 41

Felix American Pony

Sand from Fresno Canyon had slipped into Felix's boot. Grains of grit and minuscule rocks cut into the flesh of his foot. The trio had not slept since encountering the Titanoboa in Fresno Canyon. Their respective countries and organizations specially trained and selected all three men.

But even they, with their various backgrounds, couldn't wholly fight the effect of fatigue on the brain and the body.

Felix plugged his hydration kit into his mouth and sucked in the lukewarm water.

"At least this stuff is wet," he said. Despite the nastiness of the water, Felix couldn't afford to spit it out.

"*Tengo miedo,*" Radames said, "*que* if we approach this place—the exotics—that those creatures, confused by the presence of two alpha predators may act differently toward us."

"Like, attack us?" Duke asked, clutching the side stitch on his right abs as he walked.

"Not just that," Radames said. "They will be... *como se dice... indifferent.*"

"You're saying that whatever is at that exotics might act like the moose up in Montana. They'll run right over," Felix acknowledged.

It's never-ending. Felix felt the eyes of his peers looking toward him. He gave a weak smile, attempting to assuage any fear.

But there ain't no assuagin' the fear of a Titanoboa, he thought.

Dry heat continued to tear at their bodies. Sweat painted their clothing with rings of gray. But despite the terror they now faced, this shared pain had created—no—forged something else:

Friendship.

Felix rubbed his chest. He still felt agony for Mustache, Roy, and Jimbo. They had laid down their lives fighting against the terror that threatened Big Bend. Felix and his two remaining friends needed rest. They needed to stop and eat, but the memories pushed them forward.

"You sure this is the right way?" Radames asked.

"Heck," Felix chortled, "I'm kinda just makin' this up as I go."

"*Dame* the map," Radames snorted.

Felix pulled the map from his vest and handed it to the Mexican soldier. Radames held it close to his eyes and then out, like an older man adjusting to his bifocals.

"I'd say we're getting pretty close," Duke chimed.

As he studied the sweat-covered map, Radames flared his nostrils—his anger evident. "*Porque?*" Radames said, not looking up from the map.

"Because," Duke laughed and pointed, "I haven't seen too many tree houses out in the desert."

Felix looked to where Duke signaled. A pair of exotic trees with a strong base blossomed into an upturned umbrella of densely packed limbs and leaves. A finely crafted tree house sat at the bottom of the larger tree. The wood came together, composing a Queen Anne-style architectural design with a polygonal tower and conical roof. The architect had planted and weaved mesquite trees into the shingles, adorning the eclectic design with a distinct desert aesthetic. A rope bridge stretched from the tree house to the smaller exotic desert tree, where a smaller tree house of similar design rested.

"Is this a mirage?" Felix asked aloud and rubbed his eyes.

"A shared hallucination?" Radames quipped. "From the contaminated water?"

"If it is," Duke laughed, "it doesn't change its beauty."

Felix's mouth gaped, shocked by the fantastic craftsmanship displayed.

"Remember," he adjusted the sling of his shotgun. "Any animals that are around here might act different."

"Do you two have to ruin everything?" Duke said, his head back, still studying the tree houses.

"Those are..." Radames scratched his chin, "Socotra dragon trees. I studied them *en Heroico*. A Yemen-based plant..."

"Ease up, Einstein," Duke teased. "Nature is beautiful enough without your commentary."

"Guys!" Felix interjected. "We still have a mission here."

"I think we need to find a way up," Radames said.

Felix gritted his teeth at the obvious statement. He rolled his eyes.

"And I feel like that ladder right there," Duke pointed, "is the best answer."

Again, Felix's eyes went in the direction that the Japanese soldier pointed. Below the base of the larger tree house was a finely woven rope ladder.

The trio maintained security. They adjusted their long arms as they looked around the area.

Felix tilted his head back and studied the enigmatic architecture, "You two grunts ever entered and cleared a tree house?"

CHAPTER 42

Yennifer Santa-Anna

Yennifer cried out in pain. Her cries went far out into the Tapado Canyon and bounced off the Bofecillos Mountains, echoing throughout the Big Bend State Park.

"My knee," she sobbed.

Pain shot through her whole body as she pushed on her hands and knees, struggling to sit up straight.

"Oh no," she looked down at her right knee. Her feet turned one hundred degrees, with her right foot stabbing into the sand. Bile rose in her throat; she fought the urge to pass out as she saw her gnarled, contorted knee. She had grown up playing basketball and cheerleading and knew what had happened.

She had busted her ACL.

She shuddered now, thinking about when it had occurred. The Gorgon had slammed its mighty paws down on her lower body. So many factors of pain—the rugged terrain underneath her back that lacerated her flesh, the claws that tore at her knee, and the pressure of the immense weight smashing into her leg. Despite the commotion's complexity, she had heard the ligament tear.

"Why didn't it kill me?" she asked aloud. "It just left me here."

The Gorgon had spent an hour playing with her semi-conscious lover. In her disabled state, she could provide him no relief but had occasionally thrown rocks at the Gorgon—some of which had accidentally struck Oliver. Then suddenly, the Gorgon had stopped. It had slapped both paws on the ground, like a canine playing with its toy. It then tilted its head back and sniffed the air.

"*Suéltalo!*" Yennifer cried out.

But the monster didn't obey. Instead, it grabbed Oliver by the groin with its terrible saber teeth and sprinted away with the dying man in its mouth.

"Ayudameeeeeeee!" Oliver's voice grew softer as the monster dragged him through the Big Bend State Park.

Why has it so suddenly vanished? she thought.

"Ugh," Yennifer groaned as bits of Oliver's remains that she hadn't realized were dripping from her hand began dripping onto her face. "It didn't run like it was scared, but it didn't want to be here."

Adrenaline rushed through her body, feeding her muscles energy. She pressed herself up and attempted to stand up.

"No!" she cried out. Gravity hit her, toppling her over. She slammed into the ground. Her face hit a spine-covered cactus. She screamed in agonizing wails, as long needles pierced her right eye. The needle shot past her cornea, penetrating the pupil before digging into the optic nerve.

"¡Estoy ciega!" she screamed and clutched her face.

All light vanished from her destroyed right eye.

Screaming, Yennifer sat up. But while agonizing pain ravaged her whole body, it would be brief.

"You're why it ran," she said. Despite her misery, her left eye caught the horrible image before her:

The head of the great Titanoboa.

It didn't strike. It didn't need to—Yennifer had been blinded and crippled. Instead, the great snake conserved its energy. No striking. No constricting.

It spread open its mouth, descending it jaws. It shot forward, not biting but enclosing its mouth around Yennifer's legs.

Yennifer slapped her hands against the serpent's head. But the legless land-leviathan moved undeterred.

Its mouth crept forward, over her chest, pinning her arms against her head. Then, with one final push, the Titanoboa shot forward, its great mouth engulfing the screaming Yennifer.

It swallowed Yennifer whole. With indescribable pain and at a laggard pace, Yennifer was digested in the belly of the great snake.

CHAPTER 43

Felix American Pony

Felix climbed up the ladder of the tree house. A door with a locked handle was on the underneath portion of the enigmatic structure located in the Chihuahuan Desert. It was designed to be unlocked from this section and then climbed inside.

"That's pretty high," he said as he took a few seconds and scanned the world below him.

"You ok?" Duke asked through the radio.

Felix looked down at Duke, who stood at the base of the ladder. He gave an artificial smile and threw a thumbs up. Below him, the ladder stretched over twenty feet.

"I hate heights," he sighed and wrapped his legs around the rope, securing himself. He pulled a pair of bolt cutters from his vest and reached up to cut the door's lock. But to his surprise, no such lock was present.

I know there was a lock there, Felix thought. He blushed, stowed the cutters, and reached upward. He pushed the door open, grabbing the handle to make no noise.

With silent precision, he set the door against the floor. He hoisted himself up and twisted his neck to scan the area. Beautifully polished wood composed the tree house's interior. A table with a bark-covered wood base and a silver-colored pitcher made up the kitchen area.

"Here goes nothin'," Felix said, pulling himself upward.

From the corner of his eye, he saw an object jut forward. A Bowie knife rested next to his chin.

"*Que paso?*" A feminine voice cackled with a silver, musical laughter. "A Shadow Wolf caught unaware?"

CHAPTER 44

Felix American Pony

Felix glanced sideways as he knelt inside the tree house. His face burned with excitement; a whole kaleidoscope of butterflies rushed through his stomach as he felt blood rushing into his lower body. A tan hand adorned in turquoise rings clutched a Bowie knife beside his jawline.

Felix sighed and stood up.

"What's your status?" Felix's radio squawked.

The figure wielding the knife stepped forward. She tilted her head down, and her thick, black hair covered her face. With her free hand, she keyed the mic.

"He's been compromised," she whispered into the radio.

Her voice, Felix thought.

It rang with the mellow hum of an alto flute but a slight roughness in her timbre like a knife sharpened against a whetstone. Goosebumps ran down his scalp to his spine.

Locks of dark black hair crowned her head. As she stepped forward, a pair of eyes that showed an obsidian-like quality stared into Felix's soul. His stomach churned and his mouth went dry.

Her purple lips stretched into a merciless smile across olive-colored skin.

"So," she purred, trailing the Bowie knife blade down his vest, "are you going to introduce me to your friends?"

Felix sighed. He grabbed the radio and pressed the button, enabling the microphone.

"C'mon up, guys," he said, "it's safe."

CHAPTER 45

Felix American Pony

Felix watched as the other two men climbed up the ladder. He grimaced as he looked at the woman. The Bowie knife presented lethality juxtaposed to the long, beautiful feminine hair she had thrown over her shoulder, exposing her statuesque neck. Felix growled; her perfume wafted into his nostrils.

As soon as Duke saw the woman, he hoisted his shotgun.

"Drop the knife!" Duke yelled.

Radames assumed a similar posture.

"Relax!" Felix stepped forward and set his hand on Duke's shoulder.

"*¿Que?*" Radames asked.

"She's my… friend," Felix said.

"Ooooh," the woman purred, "that's a fun way to put it."

"You know her?" Duke exclaimed.

Felix felt his face redden. "She's my ex-wife."

"And she's got a Bowie knife pointed at you?" Radames asked.

"Wow," Duke said, "I don't know whether to be afraid or to be—"

"Easy there, Yūjin," Felix set a heavy hand on Duke's shoulder, "that's *my* ex-wife."

"So adorable," she said and tossed the Bowie knife up. She caught it by the handle and set it on the table. "But Felix, I can take care of myself."

"Trust me, I know," Felix replied.

"Of course, with as much as you were off at work," she blew at the strand of hair that fell on her nose, "I had to."

"The statistics of a situation are astronomical," Radames said. "How does one coincidentally encounter their former spouse?"

"It's ain't exactly happenstance," Felix said. "I'd been hearing rumors about strange occurrences in this area, so I volunteered to investigate."

"And just so we're clear," the woman said, "I knew you were in the area."

"There's no way," Felix said. "You knew this whole time and you're just now telling me?"

"Honey," she laughed. "That's called being a woman."

Felix's heart thumped against his chest as powerful and confusing emotions plagued him.

"My friends here could use some rest and some water," Felix said.

"And you think I'll help you?"

Felix sighed, "I know you'll help me. That's why I came."

It was now the woman's turn to look frustrated. This woman—this strong individual who had made a home in the fierce Chihuahuan Desert—was suddenly transformed into a damsel in distress as her vulnerability was exposed. She was compassionate. She wasn't going to turn these people away. She would help even though Felix's return had the potential for heartache.

"Tell your boys to sit down," she said.

Felix turned to his friends and pointed at the couch.

"That woman just pulled a knife on you!" Duke whispered. "How do you know she isn't going to kill us?"

"To tell you the truth, she just might, but right now... she's fixin' us grub."

CHAPTER 46

Felix American Pony

Despite Felix's dehydration, his mouth salivated at the aroma of Dejah Torres' kitchen. Sizzling beef with sautéed green chili peppers emitted smoke. Beautiful tortillas, composed of flour, sat picturesque adjacent to the meat.

"Things didn't work out between us," Felix approached Dejah Torres in her kitchen, "but your fixings always gave me an appetite."

"Too bad," she said as she grabbed salt-soaked chips from the cabinet. "You were never home to eat…"

"There's so much that I can't say," he went toward the cabinet and started looking for the silverware.

"This isn't your kitchen, Felix."

"I want to help."

"I can handle myself," Dejah gritted her teeth.

"Of course you can," Felix said. "I just wanted to lend a hand."

Dejah sighed. "The cutlery's by the icebox."

Felix nodded and moved toward it, "And by the way, how did you get an icebox up here?"

Dejah answered, but Felix said nothing, wholly focused on what he saw.

"Are you even listening?"

"Nope," he said as he pulled out a brown bucket with silver casings inside the icebox. "You got homemade ice cream?"

"Yes," she said. "Just the way she taught me…"

Felix stared at Dejah. His face was ashen.

"Felix," she said.

He breathed in a yoga-style rhythm as he worked to calm his beating heart.

"Your men need you," Dejah pulled a pitcher from the icebox. "Let's get them fed."

***

Felix watched in disgust as Duke Hattori sat at the tree kitchen table. The Japanese soldier used no utensils, instead devouring the sautéed green chili peppers with his grease-covered fingers. Felix shuddered as Duke moaned and bits of the dish dripped down his mouth. Flecks of meat decorated his chin, with remnants of the meal sprinkling the tablecloth around the plate.

"Sabe," Radames said. "The use of tools is what separates us from the animals."

"Whatever," Duke rolled his eyes. "The expression is 'finger looking good.'"

Felix laughed and looked across the table at Dejah.

"I would advise against exerting unnecessary effort, Duke," Radames said. *"Tenemos* considerable ground to cover."

"As your people would say," Duke said in between bites of a burrito, *"callaté."*

"Well," Felix said, while shoveling menudo, "it is good."

"Pienso que would be prudent engaging in strategic planning," Radames said.

Felix looked over at Dejah. The woman no longer sat at the table.

Out of my sight again, Felix shook his head.

"First things first," Felix said. "I reckon it's gonna take a spell to get ourselves ready."

"Si, pero," Radames said. "The notion of shotguns overcoming tanks is illogical."

Duke wiped his right hand on his pants, then scratched his head. "Are you sure we should be talking about this in front of Dejah?"

The trio looked around the kitchen. "I've heard of tanks crossing the border before," Dejah returned, holding papers. "And I've heard of up armored monster trucks."

"That represents *solamente* a fraction of the equation," Radames said.

"The animals have been acting strange. *Sonidos extraños."*

"What is this?" Felix asked as his ex-wife handed him a stack of papers.

"You're so easy to read," she said. "I can see you are trying to figure out why any criminal element is snooping around my house. A few months ago, someone tried to steal all my copper."

Felix's mouth gaped open. "Are you ok? Anything go down?"

Felix's stomach twisted. His heart thudded against his chest. And for some reason, despite the fear that Dejah should have had for her own safety, she looked more concerned for him.

"I'm ok," she said. "They cleaned out all the copper. Luckily, my insurance took care of it, so I didn't have to hire anyone to replace it. But now my cellar's a mess, filled with copper junk."

"You've got a cellar full of copper?" Felix asked.

She nodded, "Do you think that's why the cartel has people out here?"

Felix sat with bulging eyes, staring at the wall.

"Are you even listening?" Dejah asked.

"Sorry," he replied. "For a second there, it felt like I was back in my high school chemistry class."

"*Que?*"

Felix stared at the paper, seeing the list of all the high-end items of equipment and exotic animals that roamed her private zoo.

"Duke?" Felix asked.

The Japanese soldier didn't answer, but instead continued to gorge himself.

"Duke!"

Duke jumped from his seat, startled.

"You still got those nano-style cameras?" Felix asked.

"Yeah, just the ones that Ben didn't destroy."

"*Sabe que,*" Radames said, speaking with his signature stoicism, "statistically speaking our chances of survival appear slim. Three men facing anarchists, kaijus, and a tank present insurmountable odds."

"Probably," Felix scratched his head, thinking of the possibility of the resources displayed. "But we're going out with a bang."

CHAPTER 47

Felix American Pony

"I'd call it an improvement," Felix said. "Good ol' American ingenuity."

"But…" Duke Hattori looked around the room. "A falcon?"

Dejah held out her arm, her hand clad in a black leather glove. Perched on the glove sat a falcon with a leather halter covering its eyes.

After seeing the inventory of animals, Felix had spotted the falcon. Even if Duke's drones had been operational, they would have alerted the enemy to their position. Felix would have Dejah send out the falcon, and then they could identify the enemy using Duke's tech on the bird.

"That thing looks like it could tear me apart," Duke said as he approached the board with a black rectangular object.

"Si," Dejah said, "but I'm not going to let that happen."

"I meant it as a compliment," Duke laughed. "I'm dangerous, too."

Duke squinted as he pressed the object against the predatorial bird. No fear showed in his face, nor did his fingers shake, but nervous sweat spotted his brow.

With precision, Duke pressed the device against the falcon's chest and wrapped a collar around the back of its neck.

"Done," he said. From his vest, Duke pulled out his smartphone. The Japanese soldier held the device and inspected the screen. He gave a thumbs up. "We're up and running."

Felix pointed to Dejah, "Mind showing us this copper?"

Dejah nodded.

"Now listen here," Felix winced as he spoke to her, "I know you're willing to pitch in, but are you really up for handing your horses over? Horsemanship is in your blood—and in your heart."

"And my blood used them as weapons of war," Dejah said. "Whatever haunts Big Bend, I want it out!"

"Good," Felix said and turned to the others. "I've got a question for you guys."

Felix could see Radames and Duke looking at one another, trying to make sense of the conversation.

"What's up?"

"How well can you ride?"

CHAPTER 48

Felix American Pony

Goosebumps covered Felix's whole body as he followed his ex-wife down the tree house ladder. Hand over hand, they traveled down the ladder until they reached the Chihuahuan Desert floor.

Felix grabbed Dejah Torres' wrist. "Hey."

Dejah looked at him, and when she did, Felix's knees went weak—his knees trembled—as her eyes met his.

"Are you sure about this?"

"Is there something you're trying to say to me, Felix?" Dejah's voice was soft and powerful.

"What do you mean?"

She smiled, "Your ancestors weren't as good of horsemen as mine."

Felix's uneasiness vanished. He felt his muscles harden and he balled his hands into fists.

She's teasing me.

Felix realized Dejah didn't feel comfortable giving up her horses—he could see it in her face—and right now, she didn't want to talk.

"I guess we'll just have to see," he said.

She rolled her eyes, "Have you read our history?"

As she spoke, Duke and Radames descended the ladder behind them. Now, Dejah stood with her hands on her hips. Felix felt the heat radiating through his body at Dejah's glare.

"I think," Duke said, dusting off his hands, "this is where you say 'yes, dear' and move on."

Felix sighed, and Dejah shook her head. As the former spouses appeared frustrated, Radames and Duke laughed.

"Let me show you the cellar," Dejah said, gritting her teeth and waving Radames and Duke forward. Radames scratched his jet-colored hair, Duke shrugged his squared shoulders, and the two of them followed.

Dejah had told Felix where the equine pen was located, but the reality was that he already knew from studying the private zoo on the Internet.

Felix scratched his chin as he looked into the barn. Before him stood three strange horses. A clipboard hung against the wall. Assuming information about the beasts was on the document, he picked it up.

"Marwari, Akhal Tekes, and..." Felix stared at the clipboard. "Zorse?"

Felix read on to discover that each horse had been broken, but Dejah, despite her technical knowledge, hadn't found the time to continue their training.

"Well, hold onto your hats, folks" Felix said, staring at the breed names, "This should be interesting."

Felix gathered oats and tack and approached the beasts. First, he caught the Indian-breed creature—Marwari.

While the Marwari's magnificent beauty was evident, for a Westerner, the great horse's appearance was strange. The dapple gray Marwari had a slightly curved profile. On top of its picturesque profile were a pair of spade-shaped ears that turned inward and touched at the tips.

"Whoa!" Felix stopped, shocked as the Indian horse's ears twisted a full 180 degrees. Felix hid all uneasiness about the creature's exotic appearance and rode the horse as he knew how.

After the Marwari Felix focused his attention on the Akhal-Teke. The great Turkmenistan horse's coat shimmered with a metallic color, which could only be described as a palomino. Still, the reality is that color is the closest shade to describe it. The creature looked sculpted by divine hands from organic gold. Following a similar routine, Felix rode the Akhal-Teke until its wild fury turned into meekness.

"Now," Felix said, as he dismounted the Akhal-Teke and eyed the zebroid, "the fireworks are really going to fly."

Felix's stomach fluttered with anticipation as he gathered tack and grains to capture the hybrid animal. The zorse appeared to know its training was next. It flicked its ears behind its head and stretched forth its neck. It screeched in an enigmatic call that sounded familiar but not quite like a horse. Its zebra-like bristling mane shook left to right at its cry. It stomped its back foot and threw its tail back and forth.

"You're gonna listen to me," Felix said as he opened the gate to the round pen and approached the hybrid.

"Now, go!" Felix cracked his whip against the ground. The hybrid took off, running in the round pen. A cloud of dust shot skyward.

"Got some spirit," Felix said, watching the zorse continue its burst. "I like that."

Felix stepped forward, cracking the whip again, signaling the creature to turn in different directions. With precision, it twisted and sprinted in the opposite direction.

For the next hour, Felix trained the zorse—pushing it further and faster in the round pen. Finally satisfied, Felix put on the saddle and bridle. He took Vinyasa-style breathing to calm himself as he climbed and placed his boot-covered feet in the stirrups.

"How's he doing?" a feminine voice called.

As he adjusted his hands on the reins, Felix looked up. Dejah walked toward the round pen and rested her hands on its rails.

"I'd say, all things considered, not so bad," Felix reached up to his bandana. The zorse darted left—throwing Felix sideways. The movement was too quick for him to adjust. He rolled sideways, relaxing his body.

WHAAM!

Felix slammed to the ground. Expertly, he fell on his hip and lateral muscle. Felix moaned and sat up. Blood trickled from the corner of his lip.

"I'd say," Felix patted the blood with the back of his hand, "… we're probably gonna need a few more rounds."

CHAPTER 49

Felix American Pony

Felix looked at Dejah, who sat in the driver seat of her Toyota Tundra. The vehicle sat outside her tree house in Big Bend State Park. Beside her was the cage that contained the falcon. Pressed next to it sat a tactical, hard-case laptop.

"You sure you can handle that computer system?" Felix gestured toward the device.

"Don't worry about me," she said, patting his face.

"I know, I know you can take—"

"*Si*," she said, drawing her face closer to his. "*Pero,* I know you worry. I know you worry about me."

Felix sighed. His lips quivered as he fought to find words.

"I'll be fine, Felix. Go lay-in."

Felix nodded and stepped back, taking his hands off her truck. Dejah drove off, and dust shot skyward as she departed.

Let's get to work, he thought. Turning around, he found the zorse. He had tied the lead rope down to the branch of a mesquite tree. Felix pulled the rope free and climbed onto the saddle. Then, digging his heels into the creature's side, zorse and rider sprinted toward their objective.

CHAPTER 50

Felix American Pony

Felix dismounted the zorse and tied it down to another mesquite. The BIA agent overlooked a dried-out creek bed.

Before initiating the attack, they had sent the falcon out to gather intelligence. From the bird's attached device, they could see the repeated routes the Ripsaw took. The falcon's camera revealed the Ripsaw in constant patrols with armed men guarding its fuel point.

"There they are," Felix spied seven men dressed in what he assumed was anarchist-style garb—black hoodies, long unkempt hair, black tactical masks, with plate carriers adorning their chests. Random patches with hippie peace signs, anarchists' "As," and other assorted emblems decorated their kits.

But one symbol had been present on each uniform—a skull adorned with a black beret and black paint around its eyes and nose, a cigarette holder clenched in its teeth.

"*El Mimo,*" he whispered, recognizing the symbol.

Why was the tank patrolling?

The monsters now hunted in Big Bend. From what Felix understood, the anarchists would do better to reduce their footprint.

"Set," Felix whispered into his radio. He looked over at Radames and Duke's position. The two men had concealed themselves in heavy desert fauna, making it impossible for Felix to determine their location.

"Here we go," Felix whispered to himself.

From the two men's position, a Molotov cocktail flew through the air. Duke rose as the improvised incendiary device soared, and fired his shotgun.

BOOM

An anarchist flew back—killed instantly by the slug. Simultaneously, the Molotov cocktail crashed into the group.

"Showtime," Felix leapt up—Uzi in his right hand, tactical axe in his left.

BRRRT BRRRT

A spray of 9MM rounds sang from the Israeli submachine gun. One burning man spun in circles and, in his agony, sprinted toward Felix. Instantly, Felix swung his axe, burying the blade in his brain. The anarchists tried to reorient their attention on Felix. But as he sprayed the automatic fire and swung his tomahawk, the two other men continued their attack.

All anarchists fell to the ground. Flames from the Molotov cocktail leapt from pieces of the sparse vegetation. Smoke from the flames and the automatic fire rose from the corpses.

"Kanza! Kanza!" Felix yelled, alerting the other two men to the next part of their plan. The BIA agent holstered both weapons and sprinted back to the zorse.

CHAPTER 51

Felix American Pony

Felix American Pony jumped toward the zorse from behind. He pressed both hands on its quarters and landed in the saddle. Quickly, he reached forward and released the hybrid from the tie down.

"Hyah!" Felix called out as he dug his heels into the horse's side.

"It's coming your way!" Dejah spoke into the radio, her voice crackled over the speaker attached to Felix's vest.

"Hannibal! Hannibal!" Felix yelled into the radio, announcing the pre-determined code word and letting the others know that the Ripsaw tank was approaching. He gently tugged at the zorse's reins. From the kill zone, they rushed to the spur of the Bofecillos Mountains.

"Here goes nothin'," Felix said as he saw the Ripsaw approaching.

On cue, more Molotov cocktails were thrown before the mechanical beast.

"Distorting its view," Felix said. "Good, good!"

Duke Hattori—riding atop the Akhal-Teke—burst forward, twisting in circles. Riding in the tradition of the American Civil War bushwhackers, he clenched the reins in his teeth. He fired at the tank.

BANG BANG BANG

The slugs helplessly pounded against the tank—just like they were supposed to.

Blindly, the Ripsaw chased after Duke and his strange-colored horse.

"My turn," Felix said, digging into his saddle bag. He pulled out a device. "Let's hope your Mayan engineering holds up, Radames."

He dug his heels into the zorse. It burst forth, neighing with wild passion. The zorse and his rider ran at the tank.

"This one's for the ancestors," Felix said as he launched forward. He planted his left heel in the center of the horse's back and grabbed around the hybrid's powerful neck with his left arm. His upper body hung from the zorse—in his hand, he held the sticky bomb.

WHEW WHEW WHEW

He swung the sock like a medieval slingshot. The zorse sprinted closer to the mountain's base. Felix slammed the sticky bomb on the tracked wheels. As hot as the track, the adhesive hidden inside busted open.

The improvised device clung to the track and moved in a pattern.

BOOM!

When the track ran over the sticky bomb, it exploded.

"Tarzan! Tarzan! Tarzan!" Felix yelled.

On cue, Radames appeared in the tank's blind spot above. Radames crested the mountain with a rappel rope that connected to a harness. Snapped in with a carabiner and rope, he rappelled down the mountain.

Once close enough, he uncapped his harness and leapt.

WHAAM

Radames landed on the center of the Ripsaw, barely missing the rolling tracks. He rolled on the center. Felix hadn't wholly disabled it. With the one tread, it still crept forward. Radames yanked a shotgun from his back and aimed at the Ripsaw's window.

BANG

Glass shattered. Radames took a knee, then pulled an improvised pipe bomb from his cargo. Anarchists from inside now screamed and tried to get out. Radames sat atop the hatch. He launched forward and threw the lit pipe bomb inside the tank. He sprinted off the tank. With the skill of a free runner, the sprinter ran against the almost vertical wall of the mountain, then leapt toward the still-hanging rope.

BOOM!

The pipe bomb exploded. More screams emitted from the tank. Simultaneously, Radames caught the rope in both hands. The momentum pushed him forward—swinging him in an ape-like motion. At the apex of the arc, he released. Debris from the explosion followed him.

He flew up and back down. Expertly, Radames came down and combat-rolled multiple times, each roll taking energy out of his fall.

Felix watched. Smoke still spewed from the tank. It still crept forward.

And then down the crevasse ahead of them.

Inside, the anarchists screamed.

WHAAM!

The Ripsaw landed on its front. It rested on its nose before gravity pulled it over.

The screams changed to heavy coughs as smoke continued to fill the cabin. The cacophony of distorted breathing grew weaker.

Until finally, only human sounds remained.

The 21st century tank lay upside down, destroyed, and smoking.

CHAPTER 52

Felix American Pony

Felix pulled his binoculars from his vest as he sat atop the zorse. Lifting the binos to his eyes, he stared down into the canyon.

The Ripsaw remained motionless, with the only movement being the rising smoke.

"I don't see anyone moving around," Dejah said through the radio.

"Let's check this out, buddy," Felix said and clicked his tongue. The zebra-horse hybrid moved forward, following his command.

"What are you doing?" Dejah asked through the radio.

"Analyzin' the damage," he replied. As he approached the tank, he heard heavy coughing.

Felix tried to dismount, but when he started to move, a man crawled out of the tank.

"American Pony," the man struggled to his feet.

The zorse nervously shifted from left to right. Felix's right hand shot to his holster, drawing his Uzi.

"Ben—Andrade," Felix gritted his teeth.

"Looks like you got me figured out," Ben laughed, blood bubbling from his lips.

"You wanted to start a war between the US and Mexico?"

Ben smiled, "In a world with monsters, we figured this was the best route. We shot down the cartel's plane and let the monsters loose."

"Too bad we stopped you—"

"Did you?" Ben laughed. "We used the tank to herd the snake and the Gorgon. The tank's out of the fight. They can do whatever they want."

"But all the anarchists are dead!"

"Are they?" Ben put his hand on his bleeding side, wincing. "Even if the anarchist is dead…"

Ben shot his hand down to his waist. Simultaneously, Felix yanked the reins to one side—pulling the zorse's head out of the way. He aimed the Uzi.

BRRRT BRRRT BRRRT

The anarchist crumpled to the ground.

Felix leapt from the zorse. With an excellent isosceles stance, holding the Uzi forward, Felix stepped closer to Ben. He aimed his Israeli submachine gun at Ben's head and kicked the pistol out of his hand.

As he approached, Duke and Radames rode to his position—their horses galloping toward Felix.

"I'm good," Felix said, eyes still focused on Ben. He knelt and pushed the anarchist over.

"We'll clear the rest of the tank," Duke said. Both men dismounted and drew their long arms.

"I know what you were trying to say," Felix said to the bloody, smoking corpse. "You were trying to say that, even if we killed the anarchists, anarchy had already won."

Satisfied that Ben Andrade was dead, Felix holstered his Uzi.

If Ben had been telling the truth—if the anarchists had been herding the monsters—that meant that these two creatures were now free. Felix shuddered at the pain that a Titanoboa and Gorgon could unleash. The rugged terrain of Big Bend would allow these unchallenged predators to go undetected.

Last year, a rabid Pit Bull had killed five campers in Big Bend National Park. The Tsavo man eaters had killed over 135 people before being killed by an Anglo-Irishman. The Champawat Tiger had killed over 400 before being killed by a different Anglo-Irishman.

"How many thousands will these monsters kill?" Felix asked aloud.

Felix had killed Ben before he could finish his thought, but Felix knew what Ben had attempted to say.

The anarchists were dead, but anarchy had won.

CHAPTER 53

Felix American Pony

Felix holstered his weapon. He looked up at his friends, who stood by the smoking tank in the Big Bend.

"They're all dead," Duke said.

"So's the traitor," Felix replied and kicked at the corpse with his boot.

"Hubiera preferido," Radames said, "to have salvaged the tank."

"Welcome to the potluck, pal," Felix said, the sarcasm in his voice evident.

"They used the tank as a monster wrangler," Felix said, "and we just destroyed it."

Radames sighed, *"Nuestro* endeavors were futile."

"Monsters… cartels… El Mimo?" Felix pulled the bandana from his head and wiped his face and neck. "I reckon we never really had a chance."

"You look at the challenge—monsters, an unforgiving desert, sheer mountains," Duke said. "But you forget one thing."

"Yeah?" Felix asked. "What's that?"

"The heart of a Texan—following ol' Crockett's example," Duke said. "Those guys are outnumbered and underpowered, but as long as they breathe—they fight."

PART IV

"Passion is my compass, it guides me towards the unknown…" – Selena

CHAPTER 54

Jorge Mondragon

Jorge's face twisted in frustration as the band of mercenaries continued their march through Big Bend State Park. He looked from Brody to Gotham and grimaced.

In reality, he wasn't frustrated with Brody. He was frustrated with Gotham.

On a personal level, Jorge couldn't stand the idea of Brody. Californians were notorious in West Texas for moving in, starting a business, and then turning that profitable enterprise into a non-profit. Those fru-fru coffee shops and snobby bookstores brought in a chunk of change. Still, instead of paying local taxes, they received tax dollars. As a result, other businesses and residents were left to suffer the increased taxation.

Do I really have a duty to Brody?

Jorge looked over at Gotham. Gotham didn't say anything—he didn't have to. He seemed like a good commander. And Jorge's mind rushed to his best commander, the commander Jorge had had when he first served as a Team Leader.

"You can love your soldiers without liking them," his commander had once said.

At first, Jorge hadn't understood. But as time progressed, he came to understand. You couldn't baby your soldiers, but you had to train them hard. You had to show the tough, realistic training they needed to stay alive.

That was love; that was duty.

And without saying anything, Gotham's look of disapproval had corrected Jorge's path. His duty was to Brody. Brody deserved the protection of the Texas State Park Police.

Even if I don't like him, Jorge thought.

As he walked, continuing to follow the sign, Jorge looked back at the Californian. There, on the deadhead's black shirt, he saw in white letters:

Tempus Quartet.

Well, at least that deadhead has a good taste in music.

CHAPTER 55

Jorge Mondragon

Jorge continued walking, following the monster's sign, and traveling northeast through Big Bend.

"The trail is still hot," Jorge said.

"And so are we," Gotham said.

"*¿Que?*" Jorge asked.

"I'm saying we've been walking twelve hours. My men need some rest."

"We can't stop now," Brody sprinted to their position, somehow having overheard their conversation. "Tennyson's still out there."

"Yes, Tennyson's still out there," Gotham echoed. "And we need to be on our game when we encounter the Gorgon if we want to bring him back in one piece."

"But," Brody got within inches of Gotham's face, "I ain't stopping."

Gotham didn't take Brody's challenge. He nodded, listening to the Californian's words.

"If you feel that way," Gotham started.

"Trust him, Brody," Jorge interjected. "It's tough, but…"

"You're taking his side?" Brody asked. "I'll push by on my own. I can't stop now."

For a brief moment, Jorge stared into space, daydreaming of Brody's departure. He sighed and set his hand on Brody's shoulder.

"Trust the process," Jorge said. "Gotham knows a thing or two about hiking out in the brush."

Jorge watched as Brody looked down at his hand and then back at Jorge.

"If you say so, Jorge."

Jorge winced and pulled his hand back.

You're still not my friend, hippie, he thought. He opened his mouth to spew words of hate, but upon seeing Brody's concern for his friend, changed his mind.

"Don't worry, Brody, we'll get back on the trail."

Brody nodded and went back to Jimmy's position in the formation.

I could have been done with him, Jorge thought. *What's going on with me?*

"You know any place he can brush up?" Gotham asked.

Jorge scanned the area. "Yeah, we're next to Fresno Canyon. I know some spots."

"Lead the way."

Jorge nodded, then waved his hand to signal the group to follow him.

Before them stretched a wide-mouthed cave. This cave—a cave Jorge had seen before—no longer looked like just a hole but a dark portal daring them to enter.

This place, Jorge thought, *feels...different.*

"Is that where we are going to rest?" Brody asked and pointed at the mouth of the cave, which Jorge stared at.

"Could be," Jorge scratched his head. "But I'm nervous black bears might be in there."

"Black bears aren't grizzlies," Brody said. "They'll avoid people."

"They're still wild," Jorge replied.

"Yeah," Brody agreed, "and they have a sense of smell seven times greater than a canine. If we go near there, it'll pick up our scent and rush out."

Jorge fingered his mustache, "That makes sense."

This guy might be a veterinarian after all.

For a split second, Jorge thought to tease Brody that his distinct scent—THC and body odor—would be the most effective in scaring off a bear.

"I'll check it out," a voice said.

Both men turned. Behind them stood Bill Bosworth. On his head, he wore electronic hearing protection. Jorge recognized the device had enabled him to eavesdrop on their conversation.

"Enjoying yourself?" Jorge pointed at the active ear muffle.

"Well, yes, actually," Bill smiled. "Last time I got to clear a cave was Afghanistan."

"Go ahead, Crazy," Jorge laughed and shook his head.

Bill gave an eager thumbs up and stomped toward the cave, ensuring his footsteps carried through and allowed critters to hear his approach. On cue, a snake slithered forward. It didn't rush with the reptile's usual S-shaped motion but traveled between Brody and Jorge in a slow, indifferent manner.

"That ain't normal behavior," Jorge said.

"No," Brody replied. "It's not—"

Suddenly, the cave exploded in automatic fire. The hiss of Bill's Underbarrel flamethrower sounded.

Brody and Jorge looked at one another before sprinting toward the sound.

CHAPTER 56

Jorge Mondragon

As Brody and Jorge sprinted toward the cave in Big Bend, they were greeted by horrible sounds.

They ran into the mouth of the limestone opening and pushed inside.

"Ugh!" They were met by the smell of scorched flesh and smoke.

"Bear!" Brody screamed and pointed.

A flame-covered bear howled in agonizing growls. Its hind legs lay flat and motionless and it twisted its head back and forth. Orange sparks danced on the black fur of its neck, back, and limbs.

"Its back is broken," Brody said.

"It's on Bill!" Jorge stepped forward. He drew his Smith & Wesson XVR 460 Magnum and jammed the muzzle against the burning black bear's skull.

BANG BANG

Despite the flames, Brody yanked at the dead bear. It slammed sideways, landing on its side.

The flames leapt onto Brody's hands and he screamed in agony. Quickly, Jorge slapped at the heat, continuing to pound until the flames went out. He spun around and knelt beside the fallen man.

"What's going on?" Gotham's voice could be heard as he sprinted inside.

Jorge threw his assault pack on the ground, grabbed his hydration kit, and dumped it on Bill. The hissing flames died out, but the gun expert remained motionless.

"He's dead," Brody said. "Must have sucked up the flames and burnt up his lungs."

Jorge readied himself for CPR, throwing both legs over the man's torso and straddling him.

As he did, Gotham jumped in and pressed his fingers under Bill's jaw, searching for a pulse.

"He's gone," Gotham said and grabbed Jorge's shoulder.

The man single-handedly took on an American black bear, Jorge thought as he slowly rose to his feet.

"B-b-black bears avoid people," Brody stuttered.

Jorge's whole body trembled. He looked at Bill's burned body and the corpse of the burning, atypical creature.

Research proved that black bears had killed about seventy people since 1900, but some experts speculated that the over 400 missing persons from US National Park had fallen victim to the powerful creatures.

"Look," Brody pointed at the ground behind the fallen bear.

"That sign shows that the bear ran straight at him," Jorge's voice quaked.

"That wasn't what I was pointing at," Brody shook his head and pointed. "Look!"

Jorge followed Brody's finger. There, in the cave, lay a human corpse. The body's torso was open. The cadaver's ribs expanded open, exposing an empty shell where lungs, pectorals, and other organs had once been. The body's chest was completely gone. Bits of blood, fluids, and torn cotton cloth polluted the macabre scene. The corpse wore jeans on its lower body and a long sleeve shirt. The dead body's head was turned away from view. Jorge walked to the other side.

"My LORD," he cried out in shocked prayer.

A beautiful woman with beige skin and crowned with beautiful black locks tucked under her face stared in open-mouthed terror.

"She crossed illegally," Jorge said. "She must have done it without a guide to end up in a place this dangerous."

"It ate her," Brody said. "Bears are omnivores, and it wasn't a quick kill. Pinned her down and started tugging at the meat. Slowly— painfully—eating her organs while she still lived."

"And then it ran straight at Bill," Jorge's voice squeaked as he fought to maintain his emotions. He had gone through the Texas Game Warden Academy in Hamilton, Texas, and had studied the Big Bend black bear population.

This wasn't normal.

But this situation, however terrifying, was moot. The ecosystem had changed when the Gorgon invaded. Animals no longer viewed humans as the apex predator, but now feared this primordial predator that haunted Big Bend.

Earlier, a snake had slithered past Brody and Jorge undeterred by human presence. This American black bear had tasted human flesh and had grown mad in delight.

It wasn't the monster that had destroyed him. No, it was this place.

Bill Bosworth had been killed by this strange new ecosystem.

The Gorgon would continue to hunt and continue to kill. And even if the monster no longer posed a threat, this new and alien ecosystem did.

CHAPTER 57

Jorge Mondragon

After the proper storage of both Bill Bosworth and the woman's mutilated remains, the group headed back out of the cave. They continued traveling north through Big Bend State Park with a now-fatigued Jorge following sign.

"Don't worry about sleep," Jorge whispered to Gotham, "that wouldn't be rest—that would be nightmares."

Gotham opened his mouth to speak but only nodded instead. A beautiful young woman with a concave torso; a burning, back-broken black bear smothering Bill Bosworth; images so horrific they would have been labeled as obscene.

"I can see what Gotham meant," Brody walked beside Jorge. The Californian yawned and rubbed his eyes.

"And no, it ain't an option," Jorge growled.

"Do you read much science fiction?" Brody asked.

Jorge furrowed his brow and twisted his back at Brody. "What are you talking about, Brody?"

"I just mean, they got it all wrong."

"Who?"

"Everybody," Brody said. "Sci-fi predicts so much. This really stupid Sylvester Stallone and Wesley Snipes movie predicted Schwarzenegger's governorship, cancel culture, and social distancing."

"So, that one cartoon where everyone is drawn with yellow skin predicted—"

Brody laughed, "Yeah, but that was over thirty years. That Sly movie was just two hours and it predicted so much. But I'm trying to point something out."

"What's that?"

Brody continued to walk, and in his fatigue, his movement grew more exaggerated as he fought not to stumble. "Subgenre."

"What do you mean?" Jorge asked.

"For instance, that famous dinosaur movie, that's just a monster and survival movie," Brody explained. "But there would be so much more going on. The ecosystem, just like we saw, would act greatly different. While science fiction always gets the idea of corporations and corrupt governments taking over an operation, they forget about the cartels... the same way Pablo Escobar bought hippos, he'd be buying up dinosaurs. And HP Lovecraft, his stuff is cosmic horror. It's sci-fi that's nastier than other subgenres. Still, the reality is that cosmic horror—the fear of the unknown—would affect everything. Big Bend State Park is the most beautiful place in the Lone Star State. But, it's also dangerous. Not only do you have flora and fauna that can kill, the twists in the roads lend themselves to automobile accidents. Then you have refugees, smugglers, all traveling north as well—"

"And now we have the Gorgon..."

"Yes," Brody said. "The natural order has been changed; mankind has been dethroned."

As Brody continued to speak, Jorge studied the landscape. His eyes traced the yellow-flowered manzanilla, the yuccas, and the prickly pears. He felt the heat radiating from the soil. No longer did the plants dance from the push of a gentle zephyr; no, now the gusts of wind carried the intense temperatures onto the travelers. This new, strange gust destroyed any chance of relief from the Mercurian-like weather.

Jorge had grown up reading Louis L'Amour and watching John Wayne movies. The technicolor cinematography of those films painted this area in majestic hues. Still, from a different perspective, this environment looked similar to the geography of the Martian moons of Phobos or Deimos. But as Brody continued describing this new situation, Big Bend's landscape not only appeared alien, the entire landscape now possessed a sinister feel. The harsh desert plant life no longer just lacerated travelers; its multiple cuts forced walkers in circles, pushing them into peril by making them lose their way.

Jorge turned back to Brody and refocused on his words.

"A new king has been ordained," Brody said. "With a harsh environment in coordination with it. This environment that was already dangerous is now... *malicious*."

Jorge shivered. A Cactus Dodger cicada cried out in its high-pitched buzz-saw-like song. Other cicadas followed its lead until an entire brood sang in an unnerving choir filling the desert with a Lovecraftian-like melody.

Jorge covered his ears, trying to avoid the sound.

"You alright?" Brody asked.

"Yeah," Jorge sighed. "It's just that we're in an uphill battle."

Brody nodded. Jorge could see Brody's wistful stare, as if trying to think of a question to relieve Jorge of his current train of thought.

"So," Brody scratched his head, "do you see where this trail is taking us?"

"*Si*, the trail leads there," Jorge pointed to the great mountain in the distance. "It is taking us to El Solitario. It is taking us to the volcano."

CHAPTER 58

Jorge Mondragon

Jorge held his binoculars and studied El Solitario—the volcano overlooking Big Bend.

"Go get Tarzano," Jorge whispered to Brody.

Brody nodded and ran to the Floridian. Jorge continued to study the volcano under his lens.

"¿Que paso?" Tarzano asked, his voice wavering from extreme fatigue.

"Here," Jorge pulled the binocular strap from his neck and handed them to Tarzano. "Look at that mountain."

Tarzano brought the device to his eyes and adjusted the lenses.

"What exactly am I looking at, Jorge?" Tarzano asked, still scanning El Solitario.

"Do you see the soil underneath the rocks that looks more pink than dark?"

"Si."

"Do you see the torn plants and that upturned mesquite?"

Tarzano studied with quiet precision. "Yeah, I think I see it. What do those things mean?"

"The pink, lighter soil means it has been kicked up," Jorge said. "The overturned boulders and downed mesquite is what we call 'high sign.'"

"So, that's our route?" Tarzano pulled the binos back and looked at Jorge.

"And that's why I need you. That is El Solitario and it looks like our perpetrator went straight up that wall."

Tarzano patted the butterfly-coiled rope that he had pinned to the top of his rucksack. "It's time for me to show how I earned the ram's head."

"Yup, show us what you learned at Mountain Warfare."

Tarzano put the device up to his eyes once more. "Alright, let's get to work."

***

Tarzano ran to Gotham. Gotham collapsed the team to discuss the route and next steps in the plan. The team no longer had to move with a slow deliberate pace to allow Jorge to study the path. They had identified a further target and now had to move to it.

"I'll take point," Gotham said.

"Ugh," Tarzano grunted. *"Va despacio,* Gotham."

"What's the matter?" Jorge asked.

"Gotham over there," Tarzano pointed at their leader, "he and his buddy won the best Ranger competition."

"Making the Guard proud," Jorge acknowledged.

"Maybe so," Tarzano said, "but I'm still going to need energy to rig us up."

Jorge's stomach twisted as he thought of the grueling task of keeping up with Gotham.

"I'm a leader before I'm an athlete," Gotham said.

"Good to hear," Jorge said.

"Pero," Gotham countered, "I still gotta push."

Jorge nodded. Gotham then put his team into a file, identified the route, and started his path with the others following behind.

CHAPTER 59

The Gorgon

The Gorgon continued its rage-filled sprint through Big Bend State Park. The dying man, still in its mouth, beat against his snout with his hopeless, hate-filled strikes. The man's screams went from a rich baritone into a high treble clef with sword-like teeth pressed further into his groin. It relished the taste of blood that slid down its teeth and onto its tongue.

It wasn't afraid, but it wanted its territory. The other creature—the great snake—had never been in its region. The Ripsaw tank had kept them apart, enabling them to continue their hunt on different sides.

There was so much to hunt and kill that there was no reason for the two creatures to interact.

The Gorgon and the Titanoboa lived on the cartel leader's land. Both had escaped the plane crash. And now, in this new strange land, they had been liberated. A gust of wind swept past him as he ran. While the sun burned the area, the monster's speed was so great that despite the intense heat carried by the air to it, the wind felt cool—allowing time to recover.

But while land provided for its physical needs, something else motivated the monster.

While science says animals shouldn't be treated and studied as humans, it is unfair to believe emotions are unique to humanity. Despite the land that filled its stomach and allowed its dominance, the Gorgon still felt a pang in its heart.

A feeling similar to sorrow.

It had lost both its mate and its offspring. It was not a monogamous creature, but that didn't stop the emotional pain that stabbed its heart. Humankind had killed its kind, leaving it forever alone.

"Please!" the man in its mouth cried out. "Let me go."

The Gorgon felt the fists against its snout growing weaker. The drip of blood that touched its tongue grew slower. The monster could sense a specific emotion coming from the man.

The Gorgon slammed both feet into the ground. It spat the prey from its mouth. The gore-caked man slammed into the hot Chihuahuan Desert soil.

The monster stepped back, observing the man. Tears and mucus fell from the man's eyes, nose, and mouth. His whole body shook as he pressed his hands against the soil, pushing himself backward and away from the monster.

The monster traced its tongue against its teeth. It wiggled its snout, letting its whiskers shake. Not only could it smell this new emotion—it could *taste* it.

"I have a family!" the man sobbed.

In a canine-like motion, the monster tilted its head sideways as it observed the creature.

"I have a wife and children," the man continued to whine.

The monster didn't understand the man's words. But it didn't matter. Humans communicated verbally, but this monster communicated with its other senses.

It didn't understand the man's shaky words, but it could sense what occurred. It sat back on its hind legs, then pointed its snout skywards.

The man wreaked of this new emotion, and what could best be described as goosebumps covered the monster's flesh. It shot its head forward—nipping at the man's foot.

The man screamed in pain.

The cat-like behemoth's teeth sliced through bone, severing the foot from the leg. The scent—the taste of fear—in the man grew with ardent fervor.

The monster bit again, and again the fear grew stronger.

The Gorgon purred with excitement. The monster was resolved. It no longer had its mate or offspring. Mankind had destroyed its opportunity for love.

But this new taste—the *fear*—*this* would be its new desire.

If the beast couldn't have love, then it would create fear.

CHAPTER 60

Jorge Mondragon

Jorge grimaced as the company followed Gotham through Big Bend State Park. Gotham didn't sprint but, due to his athleticism, his natural pace was challenging.

"That volcano is dormant, right?" Brody asked.

"El Solitario?" Jorge pointed at the mountain. "That only makes it slightly less dangerous. The harsh vegetation will cut us up, and we'll have to ascend an intense incline. Once we've gone through all that, we can fight the Gorgon... at least, this sign says the Gorgon's there."

"I don't wanna sound like a subversive..." Brody said.

Despite the agony that shot through his body from the arduous march, Jorge couldn't contain his mirth.

"But I'm more worried about my friend than killing that thing."

"The best first aid is rounds down range," Jorge said.

Brody rolled his eyes. A pang of guilt tugged at Jorge's stomach.

Brody saved my life. And I've done nothing but give him grief.

He kicked at the ground as he walked. "Hey, *güey,* I never meant..."

"What's up, dude?"

"I've given you grief this whole time," Jorge looked at the Chihuahuan Desert floor. "I wanted to say—"

Ring Ring Ring

Jorge's vest vibrated. The music of Grupo Frontera sounded from his uniform. He looked down at his vest.

"*¿Que?*"

"You get a signal out here?" Brody asked. "You still have ringtones? What is this, 1999?"

Jorge pulled the phone from his vest. "Hello?" he said, putting the device next to his ear.

But no one answered.

"With all things considered," Jorge said, "getting a signal out here is still kinda weird."

CHAPTER 61

The Titanoboa

The great snake—the terrible Titanoboa replicant—slithered past the base of the Bofecillos Mountains and toward the carnage. Its serpentine form coiled and uncoiled—its predatory intent evident—as it gazed upon the blood-matted body of Ben Andrade.

The great worm stuck out its tongue—tasting the air. Ben Andrade's wounds formed a zipper-like bloody trail that ran from his navel to his throat. The snake unhinged its jaw and slithered toward the dead anarchist. Slowly—inch by inch—it consumed the body.

Feet, legs, head.

The Titanoboa's muscles contracted, slamming against the corpse. It felt its digestive fluids and muscles tear into the body and begin the process of digestion. It slithered in an s-shape fashion toward the Ripsaw tank. It swerved left to right, looking inside the wreckage.

Dead humans painted the inside in a terrible Picasso-like design. The Titanoboa pushed through, grabbed a foot with its teeth, and yanked backwards.

BAAM BAAM

As the snake-kaiju yanked backwards, the anarchist's legs slammed into the broken window. But while the destroyed vehicle presented an obstacle, the legless leviathan was too strong. The corpse body's legs snapped backwards, parallel with its torso, spilling more gore.

In a fluid motion of horrific grace, the snake pulled backwards with its teeth and coiled its massive scale-covered body around Ben's carcass. The Titanoboa's body did what it was designed to do. Just as the bioengineered snake's physical form was more massive, so was the force of its digestive enzymes. A waxy, foamy liquid ran from the snake's inside and coated the anarchist's body—melting the human cadaver.

The great snake flicked its forked tongue, savoring the taste of melting human flesh.

BANG

The monster twisted its head, searching for the sound.

BANG

A round slammed into its head and it scanned the area. There, sitting bareback on a zebra-horse hybrid was a long-haired man with tan skin and crow-colored hair. In his hand was a smoking pistol.

The reptilian didn't understand humor. For if it had, it would have bellowed in laughter and shouted, *"Is that the best you can do?"*

Yet, it did understand intimidation.

The Titanoboa replicant coiled its body underneath itself and rose twenty feet into the air. It bared its teeth—acid-like juice dripped from its fangs—covering the soil in terrible drops of slime.

BANG

The man fired again. The snake's great scaled hide gripped together on impact, deflecting the small caliber threat.

A feeling similar to anger coursed through the reptile.

"You wanna ride, snake," the rider said, "then let's roll!"

BANG

The man fired again—this time the bullet slammed into the beast's mouth. Pain seared through the snake, making its fury even greater. It reoriented, swinging its head side to side and looking for its challenge.

The man tugged at the reins, forcing the equine away. He kicked his feet into the zorse's side and a dust trail shot skyward as the pair sprinted.

The snake hissed, then shooting its body forward, it pursued.

CHAPTER 62

Jorge Mondragon

Jorge breathed in for four seconds and held it for four seconds before exhaling for the same amount of time. He stood at the bottom of the dormant volcano, El Solitario, and stared skyward. Jorge Mondragon had served with pride in the 1st Battalion, 143rd Airborne Infantry Regiment amassing over sixty jumps. Then as a Park Police Officer, he had climbed through the rugged mountains. However, unbeknownst to others, Jorge Mondragon was somewhat scared of heights.

He knew he wasn't the only one. Jorge had read about men during the Korean War who *hated* heights but longed to be Airborne Rangers and had ignored their own phobias to volunteer.

From the corner of his eye, he saw Brody. The Californian had already pulled on his harness and begun his ascent.

Man, I hate heights, Jorge laughed. *But I don't want Brody to know that.*

He pulled out his tactical gloves and fitted them onto his hands. Then, pushing away all doubt, the Park Police Officer started his way up. Because of the sheer vertical ascent, he climbed on all fours. It wasn't steep enough to be considered traditional rock climbing, but its rough rise was similar to an obstacle course.

Hand over hand, Jorge climbed. As he worked, the fear subsided and was replaced with an intense focus on the task. The euphoria of physical training created a sense of excitement in him, and Jorge found himself content and happy as he climbed the limestone mountain.

Jorge looked sideways. He led the group as the first one up the mountain. They had assumed risk with no real security; their analysis included the monsters rather than human and criminal counterparts. But Jorge had lived through COVID. And just like everyone else, he had watched the Joe Exotic documentary.

Exotic animals attract dangerous people.

He patted his pistol—the gold-colored Smith & Wesson XVR 460 Magnum, sheathed in a QRS holster strapped to his side with an additional strap attachment that ran around his leg. He thought of how he'd draw his weapon against potential attackers. The slung long arm would take too long to retrieve. He'd have to steady himself and draw his pistol if he got into a mess.

"I hate not knowing," Jorge spat as he climbed.

His pistol, from years of training, had been perfected. He had trained it so long and had been demanding in his training that he couldn't do it wrong. But now, he climbed in a modified position and, instead of the Austrian-designed pistol, he carried the hand cannon he had chosen to kill the monster.

Jorge bit his lip and grunted. Law enforcement officers excelled at visualizing worst-case scenarios. As he climbed El Solitario, he had to concentrate on his hand and foot placement and think of how to respond to a contingency.

How do you shoot a bad guy when you're climbing uphill?

"Reaching the top," a voice said through the radio.

Jorge twisted his head, looking at his peers. He saw Tarzano, now standing at the top. The Floridian Guardsman pulled out his climbing equipment.

"Almost there," Jorge smiled and, with renewed energy, continued his ascent.

From the corner of his eye, he saw Gotham increase speed.

"I see how it is," Jorge yelled at his fellow paratrooper.

Gotham looked over at Jorge. He smiled, then began his climbing sprint upward. Dust and sediment fell behind Gotham as he moved. Likewise, Jorge pushed through and climbed.

"Almost," Jorge panted, "there—"

Suddenly, a high-tenor scream broke out. The terrible cry echoed down the volcano and onto the Chihuahuan Desert. Jorge turned his head.

Below him, he saw Brody—pinned against the mountain and cradling his left hand against his chest.

"It bit me!" he cried.

Jorge's eyes bulged.

There, beside the Californian, was a Trans-Pecos copperhead. It coiled up, its diamond-shaped head eyeing Brody for another attack.

A pour of nervous sweat shot out from Jorge's pores. The sweat and his regular perspiration created a distinct, unfavorable odor.

Jorge released his grip on the mountain, skidding downward. As he did, he walked forward—allowing himself to fall at a downward angle. While still moving, Jorge yanked out his Smith & Wesson XVR 460 Magnum.

He oriented it at the serpent. The arching snake redirected his attention. It shot out—aiming at Jorge's outstretched hand. It bore its fangs.

BANG BANG BANG

Jorge squeezed the trigger three times.

The snake continued forward, even as rounds shot through its body. In bullet time, it inched closer to Jorge's hand.

BANG BANG BANG

The Trans-Pecos Copperhead's skull exploded. Fragments of gore, bone, and venom slammed against the mountain. Sediment exploded from the scene and rolled downward. The rush of adrenaline now faded from Jorge, no longer in need.

But as he began to calm, Jorge lost grip and slid downward.

"Watch out!" he cried to Brody.

Seeing his friend sliding down the mountain, Brody tried to move out of the way, but Jorge slammed into him. Brody screamed as both men fell down El Solitario.

CHAPTER 63

Jorge Mondragon

The two men continued to slide down El Solitario. Somehow, Jorge holstered his pistol. He grabbed Brody's collar with his right hand as they slid downward.

"Hold on!" he shouted.

As they moved, Jorge spied a juvenile mesquite tree. He wasn't sure if it would bear both of their weight, but it could at least slow down their descent. He shot out his left hand and snagged the mesquite.

"Argh!" Jorge groaned as he gripped the base of the tree with his left hand and clutched the injured Brody with his right.

Brody twisted around and climbed toward the tree. Jorge sighed as he felt the weight released from his grip.

"I'm alright, Mondragon," Brody said, still clutching his arm.

"You're bit!" Jorge shifted his body weight and moved to his feet.

"But my friend," Brody replied, still gripping his bite with his free hand. "He's up there and he's in trouble."

Jorge studied Brody, "Well, my friend is right here and he's snake bit. We gotta get you help."

Brody nodded and pointed again, "Tarzano..."

Jorge sighed.

"You're bit," Jorge repeated and stared at his friend, a man undeterred by the poison in his body.

As if on cue, a black static rope dropped between them. Jorge looked up. At the top of the mountain, Tarzano had anchored the static bed rope and now pointed at it with emphatic gestures.

"Click into the rope!" Tarzano cupped his mouth with his hands and yelled. "I got the anti-venom! Get him up here!"

Jorge nodded, grabbed the rope, and tied the end to his harness. He inserted the static line into the black aluminum alloy descender. Next, he grabbed the jumar from his belt.

"Alright," he grabbed onto Brody, "let's get you up there."

Brody nodded and, with his good hand, grabbed onto Brody's tactical vest. Jorge clicked the jumar into the static line and began his ascent.

CHAPTER 64

Jorge Mondragon

The mountain wasn't steep enough to rely solely on the ascent device, but it helped. Jorge and Brody could now stretch out their legs against the mountain, furthering the distance of each step. Brody leaned against Jorge with one hand and clutched his bitten hand against his body. With long strides, he alleviated Jorge's burden.

"Almost there," Jorge grunted to his friend. From the corner of his eye, he saw Brody look up.

At the top of the mountain, Gotham stood with one hand out, ready to help pull Brody up. Tarzano stood beside him, managing the rope.

Lactic acid tore at Jorge's legs as he stepped and his forearms as he worked the jumar ascent device.

"Finally," he grunted.

Gotham reached down, grabbing Brody's shirt. He yanked, pulling Brody up to him. As soon as he did, Tarzano almost tackled him—squatting down beside the now supine position of the Californian. He detached the attached case on his leg and reached his hand into it.

He scrambled both hands into the bag and retrieved a white plastic vial with a red lid. The words "Crofab" were written on its body.

Snake anti-venom, Jorge thought.

Tarzano then grabbed a syringe from the bag and kneeled over. He prepared the needle.

"Tear open his shirt," Tarzano ordered, "above the bite."

Gotham drew his knife and cut at Brody's shirt above his wrist. With a syringe in hand, Tarzano plunged the medical device straight into the crook of his elbow—stabbing the needle into the median cubital vein.

"Youch!" Brody screamed out.

Jorge sighed and wiped the sweat from his forehead. "Shut up, hippie," he teased. But he was relieved to hear that Brody still felt pain in his arm. That meant the tissue wasn't all numb or dead.

Tarzano reached back into the bag, pulled out a bandage, and wrapped Brody's wrist in white gauze with fantastic speed.

"You're lucky, Brody," Jorge said as he unhooked himself from his harness. "That anti-venom is too expensive for normal knuckle-draggers like me. You had the well-funded mercs running with you and they could afford it."

"That is normally administered through an IV drip," Tarzano said. "So, Brody, make sure you are drinking water."

Brody looked at Jorge and offered a weak smile, "I wouldn't say I'm lucky, *friend-o*."

Jorge sighed, "I reckon if I was in your position, I wouldn't say that either."

"Depends on your definition of luck," Gotham said.

Jorge turned his attention to the Dark Waters leader and saw Brody try to do the same.

"What do you mean?" Jorge asked.

"*Allá*," Gotham pointed downward.

Jorge gasped for air from the exertion. He then walked toward Gotham's position, pulled his binoculars from his vest, and looked where the leader pointed.

"The sign leads to that," Jorge sighed.

There, below them, was a half-demolished 727 airplane.

"No," Gotham said, shaking his head. "*Everything* points to that."

CHAPTER 65

Jorge Mondragon

Jorge looked over his shoulder as he stood at the lip of the volcano of Big Bend State Park. Beneath his legs and trailing behind him like a tail was the black static rope. He held a gloved hand behind him as a brake hand.

"You can spend your whole life in Big Bend," Jorge said, "but this land will still surprise you."

Calling out his rappelling commands, the Texas State Park Police Officer started his descent.

Concentrate on Big Bend, Jorge thought. The Gorgon had made the land his realm, but its beauty could not be denied. The park's flora and fauna now seemed pitted against them, but still, in its beauty, Jorge found strength.

His feet slammed into the sheer rocky wall as he bounded downward. In five good bounds he made it down the cliff and onto the volcano's floor. The desert had always been dangerous, but it had also been alluring. The golden sun glowed against the beige sheer wall.

The park might have served a dark master, but the sun still rejuvenated all life with its solar rays. The heat stung his body, but the light still gave him hope.

Jorge hit the bottom. He unhitched himself from the belay system and cupped his hands to his mouth, "Off belay!"

"Belay off!" Tarzano answered.

Jorge turned around, unslung his long arm, and charged the carbine. He adjusted the weapon so it was slung against his chest.

There, Jorge looked toward the broken airplane. The sun no longer strengthened Jorge, the golden rays now blocked.

The park might have been its realm, but this place—El Solitario—had become the monster's lair. The great natural castle now belonged to the Gorgon replicant and covered the land in shadow.

But despite the overpowering darkness, Jorge and his band persevered. The squad pushed forward.

CHAPTER 66

Jorge Mondragon

The blistering heat radiated off El Solitario's dormant lava bed. Through the pain, Jorge and the others walked, step by step, drawing them closer to the down and broken aircraft.

"We'll clear this," Gotham said. "FM 7 dash 8, Battle drill 6."

Jorge nodded and readjusted his long arm as they inched closer. He toyed with the strap of his shotgun, getting it at the perfect length so the butt of the stock fitted against his shoulder.

Soldiers and cops were both tactical professions but vastly different. Soldiers were trained to seize ground and, as a result, enter and clear a room—pushing in with speed and overwhelming violence of action. Law enforcement officers were different; they were *responding* to a problem. Cops could also be much older than soldiers, so sprinting in a room might not be the best answer.

But this group—this band of Jorge, Tarzano, Gotham, and an injured Brody—didn't have time for a slow, methodical approach.

"Brody," Gotham said. "Let us clear the area, then bring you to help us look for Tennyson."

"Knees and elbows," Jorge said aloud. "If anyone besides Tennyson is in there, they're getting put in the dirt."

If there were any cartel men in there, they were the true believers—criminals whose brutality matched their professionalism.

"Let's start getting tighter," Gotham said.

With the instinctive behavior engrained into them from their military backgrounds, the three trigger-pullers acted. They bunched up in their formation until they were touching. They stepped toward the side of the aircraft. Gotham took point, then Tarzano, then Jorge. Jorge pressed his vest-covered chest against Tarzano's back. Once set, he reached up and gripped Tarzano's shoulder, then Tarzano did the same.

The trio sprinted forward into the busted service door. Gotham went in a controlled push, then Tarzano, and then Jorge.

Gotham took the left side of the area inside, Tarzano the right, and once inside the aircraft, Jorge cleared the open space in the middle.

"Clear!" Jorge said. He stifled a gag as an abhorrent odor stung his nostrils. He gritted his teeth, fighting to keep the smell out of his mouth.

When Jorge was a kid, his elementary class visited the El Paso Zoo. The staff had given the students a tour of the area and they'd seen the tools and equipment that had been in the rooms and storage areas adjacent to the animal pens. The tail section reminded Jorge of that tour and the weird smell of something having lived in there. The empennage was smashed, with the Gorgon's distinct prints pressed against the metal.

"I've never been able to cut a sign like that before," Jorge laughed.

"This room is clear," Gotham whispered. "Regroup, we'll hit the cockpit."

Maintaining good muzzle awareness, Jorge lowered his shotgun and redirected toward the cockpit. The group closed in again until they pressed against one another.

"Jorge," Gotham said. "You're third in the stack."

Jorge knew what that meant: he was the one who opened the door. "Roger that, buddy," he said before breaking off from the group. He tiptoed beside the door and grabbed the handle. He hunkered down and looked at Tarzano and Gotham, who were stacked in front of the door.

Gotham nodded and Jorge flung the door open.

With expert precision, Gotham pushed in, taking the right side of the cockpit. Tarzano followed in, clearing the left. Jorge moved in and cleared the middle.

"Clear," Jorge said.

Broken glass littered the cockpit's floor. The vessel's instruments were destroyed—twisted into unrecognizable mechanical debris. An open notebook lay on the detritus-covered station.

"Ugh," Tarzano spat. "Didn't think you could get a worse stank than the other room."

"Brody!" Gotham called up. "You're up."

Jorge listened as Brody ran inside—his feet banging against the aircraft floor. He watched the injured man enter the cockpit from the corner of his eye.

"What's up, guys?" Brody panted, still clutching his wrapped hand.

"Yeah, *pero*," Jorge said, "*this* smell is familiar."

"*Si*," Tarzano nodded, "*tiene el odor de sangre*."

Gotham grunted, clearing his throat, but Jorge knew what it meant. It meant their personal timing and bedside manner needed to be adjusted.

"What does that mean?" Brody yelled. "What Tarzano said...."

Jorge winced. While Brody didn't understand Spanish, he must have read their body language and understood the message they had attempted to convey.

"*Sangre?*" Brody shook his head left to right, looking through the cockpit. "Why did he say that? What does that mean?"

Jorge rubbed his chest as a feeling of guilt knotted his insides. He looked at Tarzano and then at a tight-lipped and disappointed Gotham.

"Why are you ignoring me?" Brody asked. "*Sangre*? He said *sangre*! What does that mean?"

Jorge spied on Gotham. The Dark Waters leader slung his long arm, adjusting the strap so it wouldn't flop against his chest. He then opened his mouth to speak. Gotham was a good leader, but it wasn't his responsibility to tell Brody what had happened. Not only did Jorge have legal authority over this park, but Brody was also his friend.

It was his job to tell him.

"It means…" Jorge interrupted. He closed his eyes, trying to think of how to give this news to Brody. "This room stinks. He said this room stinks."

"Sangre means that?"

Come on, buddy, Jorge thought, *can't you make this easy for me?*

"No," Jorge shook his head. "He was saying this room smells like *sangre*… like *human sangre*… he's saying this room smells like blood."

CHAPTER 67

Tennyson's Written Testimony:

This is the written testimony of Tennyson. My fingers tremble as I compose this document, for I fear it to be my last. My name is Tennyson Johnston. While I do not believe that THC consumption leads to addiction, I fear my life has been wasted not in its consumption but in the eternal pursuit of its purchase. In my lifetime, I was applauded for my written skills. And now, it appears my last hours will be the first I demonstrate this hidden skill.

I was educated in the finest Californian parochial schools. Still, a nun—Sister Wilima Rogers—educated at St. Gregory University of Shawnee, Oklahoma, sharpened my skills. But alas, whilst she did arm me, my skills with the written word have remained dormant.

This trip—the journey to Big Bend State Park—was one of discovery. While the reader of this document will assume my intent was further sensory exploration through controlled substances, that assumption, though reasonable, would be incorrect.

Our exploration was one of science. I was instantly enamored when I saw the images of Big Bend State Park. Its admiration is not limited only to the artist. Its enigmatic beauty garnishes praise from geologists, zoologists, botanists, adventurers, and mountaineers. Colors of the chromatic scale, known only to the beautician or physicist, can be seen here. Never before have I witnessed such a coupling of peril and beauty. The jagged limestone walls of the Bofecillos Mountains inspire the artist's quill, but undoubtedly, thousands have perished in that landscape. But despite the mortal threat, Big Bend beckoned us.

From there, we ventured into the park, snaking along the Farmer-to-Market road. But while I was still a foreigner to these parts, my gut told me something was amiss. As we continued east, we discovered hundreds of cattle walking along the road. Most animals fear man and, even if they have no fear, they typically have some sort of aversion to our kind. But these bovine beasts had no such apprehension.

Soon, to our horror, we discovered why. From my time here, I now know what it is—a Gorgon Synapsid. Following the techniques described in Jack Horner's book and fueling the unlimited funds from drug cartels, scientists and engineers manipulated the embryonic cells of modern-day fauna and created the monster. Like a modern cat, it gripped me and dragged me back here to its lair, El Solitario—the great volcano overlooking Big Bend.

In this aircraft, I discovered its secrets. The question: how did this monster get here?

In this miserable lair, I discovered the answer. Pablo Escobar had bred hippopotamus in Columbia. Following his example, coupled with new biotechnology available, Mexican drug lords naturally worked to own this primordial beast.

I was not alone here. No, the aviator—a distinguished criminal smuggler from the infamous Albuquerque Air Force—remained alive. He informed me of the genesis of this monster.

But there is something strange about organized crime. While there is chaos in my home state of California, interestingly, it was never the haven of organized crime like New Orleans, Las Vegas, Chicago, or the entire eastern seaboard. So, my pen trembles as I write the words. Mafias and cartels respect order. While history shows their barbarism to be on par with historical figures such as Hirohito, generally, they respect order. Since the 1980s, cartels have worked to prevent this open violence across the border. Cartels have even detained those who have caused harm to Americans and presented them to US authorities.

The aviator wanted me to know that his cartel never intended for this event. He acknowledged the illegal flight of a civilian aircraft flying through Presidio County. Still, the drug lord's creatures had been safely kept inside the plane.

The aviator revealed to me that a band of anarchists led by the terrorist El Mimo shot down the aircraft to create chaos that would lead to conflict between the two great republics of Mexico and the United States.

We now sit here, nursing our wounds and recording this bizarre history. Throughout my life, I have questioned my sanity and the effects played upon my brain by illicit consumption. But now, as I search for the truth—what happened here?—I question my own sanity more than I ever have in my existence.

CHAPTER 68

Tennyson's Testimony Continued

As the aviator and I worked to better understand the situation, I came to the grim realization of the imminence of my death. I fear that during the rough transportation to El Solitario, I was the victim of a blood transfusion from the Gorgon replicate. I must acknowledge that, inside my body, a new zoological disease—one that could rival even HIV—now breeds. HIV was transferred from Congolese chimpanzees and grew to devastate the entire planet. How much worse is the prion that dwells in the blood of a cartel-engineered monster?

Talking with the smuggler, I learned that the Gorgon was not alone. Another female—much smaller in stature—escaped, as well as a creature that fills me with awesome fear as I pen these words. A great snake—an anaconda whose embryonic cellular structure was manipulated by the cartel's bio-engineers—designed to replicate the great Titanoboa.

These monsters now freely haunt this beautiful land. They claim this terrain as home. As I write in this notebook, I have walked to the rear of the aircraft. I search for medical treatment for the smuggler, as all his available resources are now gone.

It seems impractical, but I am duty-bound to relay these immediate events. As I left the aviator, suddenly the whole aircraft shook. I heard a massive explosion as metal, glass, and pieces of the cockpit were destroyed under the massive weight of a monster. My whole body shook as I realized what had occurred: the Gorgon had brought us back to its haven—alive so that, when hunkered, it could not only eat but sharpen its predatorial skills. Despite my trepidation, I grabbed an axe that I had found in the rear and sprinted toward the cockpit.

Inside, I found no living thing, but a hollow shell of the aviator's former workspace. This furthered my fear. The monster had been able to break through, rip the contrabandisto from his place, and leave no visible trace.

But while I saw no evidence, my ears were not so fortunate. I could hear the agonizing screams:

"He's torturing me!" the man screamed. "Please, kill me!"

I shudder as I recount this event. I heard a massive "snap" not unlike the breaking of a wooden pole. While my mind instantly guessed what had occurred, I found relief from the agonizing choir of pitiful wails.

Initially, I heard the sound similar to a canine suddenly bursting into its meal, consuming nutrients with animalistic fury.

But then it stopped.

And I knew what that meant. The monster remembered its other prey—its other plaything—the monster remembered me.

A silence has shocked my whole body. Goose bumps cover my flesh.

I believe—no, I know—the monster now stalks toward my position.

I stifle my breathing, trying to hear its approach. But despite its massive frame, the feline-like monster treads silently. Only my soft, almost non-existent breaths can be heard.

But hark.

No, I hear, the subtle press against the rocky soil outside.

It is near.

The monster breaks into the cockpit.

It

[Unintelligible scratches mark the bottom of the notepad]

CHAPTER 69

Jorge Mondragon

"My bro is dead," Brody howled as he held the notebook. He fell downward, both knees smashing into the debris-covered cockpit floor.

Jorge rushed forward. From his time in law enforcement training, he knew the psychology of the situation. Grabbing Brody and hoisting him back to his feet wouldn't be appropriate. Still, despite his training—despite the experience that had hardened him—Jorge's heart twisted as he watched his friend's emotional turmoil.

"But I don't understand," Gotham lowered his weapon and scratched his head. "Why is there no blood?"

"It's called a *papillae*," Brody sobbed.

"Papi—"

"*Papillae*, it's a Latin word. Literally means 'nipple.' They are the spines on a cat's tongue," Brody grunted, clearing his throat. "The Gorgon has rough scaly skin but looks and acts much like a mountain lion. Its tongue is covered in rough spines. It must have licked the floor clean."

"From my time working here in Big Bend," Jorge interjected, "I can tell you there typically isn't much evidence left. Wild animals don't leave blood spatter the way humans do."

"Except you can read sign," Gotham said. "Even those monsters can't hide from you."

"Is that what happened?" Brody turned to Jorge. Jorge's stomach continued to tighten. "Can you see sign even in here?"

Heavy is the head that wears the crown, Jorge thought. While at Big Bend, he'd become an excellent tracker. And what Brody had said—the monster licking the spatter dry—was evident in what he saw on the ground. There wasn't a straight print the way there would be on the desert floor. Instead, there was transference from objects from one area being carried over to another. And just as Brody had said, he saw a semi-white colored, organic-looking thing that dug into the cockpit's carpeted floor. Bits of the carpet were torn up, matching Brody's description of the papillae.

"I'm sure we looked like two losers," Brody said. "Two hippies traveling to Texas, stinking up your park with THC..."

"That ain't true," Jorge replied, pointing at the notebook. "He wrote that as he died... as he sacrificed himself, so that others could know what we're up against."

Jorge watched Brody wipe his eyes with the back of his hand, trying to rid himself of the tears.

"Give me the bang stick," Brody said.

"What?" Jorge laughed at the thought of a hippie wielding the nuanced weapon.

Brody stepped forward and took the lance-like weapon from Jorge. Jorge furrowed his brow as he watched Brody take the bang stick and inspect it.

"Do you even know how to operate that?"

"No, not yet," Brody said, his eyes never leaving the tactical tool. "But I figured you'd teach me."

Jorge sighed, "Of course I'll teach you."

"Sounds good," Brody said. "And then we will teach them."

"Teach them… as in, teach the Gorgon?"

"Yes," Brody stood, holding the bang stick in hand.

"What's that? How can you train a forty-foot monster?"

"With this," Brody held up the weapon. "They have seen that men can be victims..."

"And now?"

"We show them that men can also draw blood," Brody said.

PART V

"Texas has yet to learn submission to any oppression, come from what source it may." - Sam Houston

CHAPTER 70

Jorge Mondragon

The broken aircraft quaked. Jorge gripped the back of the aviator's seat, balancing himself. Tarzano, Gotham, and Brody all reacted in a similar manner. Looking through the broken window, he saw El Solitario.

"It's coming home," Jorge whispered.

"Well, just call me Goldilocks," Brody charged the bang stick. Gotham and Tarzano scanned different areas, looking for potential threats.

CRASH

Shards of glass from the half-broken windshield exploded. Gotham grunted as splintered shards tore into his exposed flesh.

The great Gorgon replicant's snout burst through the wreckage. It was closest to Gotham—so close he couldn't draw his long arm up. He drew his revolver—the Chiapa Rhino—and emptied an entire magazine. The Gorgon dug his snout underneath Gotham's vest and threw his head up. Gotham flew through the air before slamming against the wall and falling into the floor.

BANG BANG BANG

Orange blasts exploded from the group's weapons. The Gorgon howled in pain and yanked its head back.

The whole aircraft shook. Jorge fell sideways. He slammed his long arm against himself and thumbed his weapon to safety. He grunted as his head bounced against the floor. He jumped—adrenaline pushing him through the pain.

WHAAM WHAAM

"What's he doing?" Jorge asked, rubbing his gore-caked head.

"He's hitting the aircraft," Brody panted, "trying to—"

Jorge and the others were thrown into the air as the aircraft tumbled sideways. Debris, mechanical pieces, and tools all tumbled in a circular motion. Jorge cried out as bits of the vessel penetrated his flesh and the aircraft tumbled down El Solitario.

CHAPTER 71

Felix American Pony

Felix leaned forward as the zorse continued to bolt onward. Wind zipped into Felix's face as they approached El Solitario. He whipped his head behind. The Titanoboa still pursued. Its black scaled face showed hungry eyes as it slithered left to right. Felix shuddered and ripped his head away, looking forward.

What is that? Felix thought as a metal hunk rolled, side-over-side down the volcano. Behind it, the great Gorgon replicant swatted its massive paw like a domesticated cat enjoying a plaything.

Is that the downed airplane?

Unaware that his friends had reached the Gorgon's lair, Felix found it strange that the monster would destroy its physical home. But despite the oddity, he still had a job to do and he needed to get as close to the Gorgon as possible.

This is why we came here, he thought.

The plan was simple:

Get the Titanoboa and the Gorgon to kill one another.

Using the drone attached to the falcon, they had located the Gorgon's position and lair.

But how many must die?

Felix glanced over his shoulder. The great serpent still pursued. He gritted his teeth and steered the zorse straight at the Gorgon.

CHAPTER 72

The Gorgon

The Gorgon chased behind the crashed airplane, swiping its massive claws. Gravity and chaos made the ascent down El Solitario perilous, but its strength and feline-like agility made its travel easy. It was a human description of its emotion, but the monster felt joy. The air whipped past its face, alleviating some of the heat.

But suddenly—the sense of joy stopped. It clung its claws into the mountain. It squatted its haunches downward, slowing its descent. Dust shot skyward. Bits of gravel and sediment went outward. The plane continued its descent.

The humans—those trapped in the plane—were not alone. Now, a long-haired man traveling on a horse-like beast sprinted toward him. The monster salivated; long gobs of spit ran down its fangs.

But the man wasn't alone either. Behind him was the great Titanoboa.

Rage filled the monster.

The serpent wasn't supposed to be here. There was enough food in its own territory.

Planting its front paws into the ground, the beast howled a warning to the slithering threat. The Titanoboa was caught unaware. The snake's eyes darted from the man and its equine-creature to the Gorgon. With indescribable speed, it coiled up. It then launched its head skyward, two stories in the air. It bore its fangs and hissed.

The snake had no right to be in the Gorgon's territory. Yet, the Titanoboa didn't seem to care.

The Gorgon shivered as the rough, pachyderm-like skin of its neck stood upward.

No retreat would be initiated by either monster.

The Titanoboa hissed.

The Gorgon roared.

The two abominations rushed at each other.

CHAPTER 73

The Gorgon

The Gorgon—open mouthed—smashed into the Titanoboa. It fell backwards and launched its tail upward and around the Gorgon's midsection. The Gorgon opened its snout and snapped its jaws. Saliva flew through the air. The Gorgon missed.

An indescribable pressure tightened around its midsection. Blood rushed to its eyes. Its eyes bulged in pain. The Titanoboa squeezed the Gorgon's midsection. The snake danced its head in a terrifying rhythm and flicked its forked tongue. But the Gorgon was clever. As the snake focused on its snout, the Gorgon shifted its right paw.

WHAAM WHAAM

The Gorgon slammed its massive right paw into the Titanoboa. Its claws dug in, penetrating the armor-like scales. All five nails shot past the organic shield and into its coiled muscle.

The Titanoboa hissed in terrifying and miserable tones. Only slightly, it released its grip.

Despite its exhaustion, the Gorgon shot forward—freeing itself from its enemy's grasp.

Both monsters tumbled downward. Sand, debris, and sediment shot skyward, forming tree-sized dust clouds. Over and over, they tumbled as they rolled down. As they fell, the Gorgon struck again. It threw its paw against the great serpent. Again, the claws dug into snake-flesh. But this time, the Titanoboa didn't cry out. It struck.

Its fangs sank into the Gorgon's shoulder. But the serpent was cunning. The descent impacted them both. The Gorgon howled in pain and with each tumble—each roll downward—the fight grew in the Titanoboa's favor. Finally, they landed at the base of the volcano, ramming into the aircraft.

The Gorgon felt its body grow weaker. Blood dripped from its shoulder. The intense pressure returned to its body. Oxygen and blood drained from the monster.

The Titanoboa was victorious.

The Gorgon was dying.

CHAPTER 74

Felix American Pony

Felix's whole body shook as he sat atop his ride, watching the two monsters fight. The beasts continued the melee as they descended El Solitario. Despite his trembling, the zorse didn't take advantage of its frightened rider. Instead, it remained motionless, waiting for Felix's next command. Felix reached down, petted its neck and mane.

"You're scared too, huh?"

Over the commotion, he heard what sounded like moans coming from the aircraft. Before he had committed to the baited ambush, Felix had observed the group via their improvised surveillance equipment entering the aircraft. It had been to his horror to watch the Gorgon chasing it down the volcano.

"Gotham!" Felix yelled and leapt from the zorse and sprinted toward the downed vessel.

At the rear, he saw the bloody forms of Jorge Mondragon and Brody limping from the wreckage.

"Are you guys alright?"

"I'm trying to get Brody out," Jorge coughed. "I don't know about the others."

"Roger that," Felix replied. "Get your guns up and oriented on the monsters. I'll go get them out."

Felix studied the inside. His mind rushed back to the brutal obstacle course he'd completed at the BIA course in Artesia, New Mexico. "So, this is why we did so many obstacles courses? For such a time as this."

The aircraft was twisted on its side, and a beam-like object running down the middle served as the first immediate obstacle. Felix took a step back and studied a potential entry point.

"Got it." He reached, grabbing the beam as high as he could. He then pressed his feet against the debris that formed a solid wall. Pulling with his hands and walking with his feet, he maneuvered over the obstacle and into the more open space of the aircraft.

WHAAM WHAAM

Felix heard the smack of metal on metal.

"Gotham!" Felix yelled.

WHAAM WHAAM

Felix yelled again.

"We're back…" a voice said, a New York city accent growing stronger with fatigue. "Back here, Felix."

Dust from unidentified material blanketed the air. Still, Felix pushed through to the voice.

Gotham stood, his blouse ripped from his body, displaying his Olympian-like build. Sweat and blood ran from a cut on his head, illuminating his muscles.

"Tarzano!" Gotham panted. "He's trapped in there."

"Why are you swinging that axe?" Felix asked. "You might hit him."

"He's in bad shape," Gotham panted and swung again. The metallic obstacle split. He pushed up on the metal, Gotham's whole-body trembling from exertion. With fatigue, he fell to the ground.

Felix knelt beside him. "Literally, passed out from exhaustion," he said aloud, checking on Gotham. Seeing he was fine, Felix looked up. Through the haze, he found him.

He saw Tarzano's supine form.

"How am I looking?" Tarzano choked.

"Agh," Felix gulped, "not that bad."

But, Felix was lying. Tarzano lay on his back on the crumpled metal floor. His blood-soaked hands covered his exposed stomach. His abdomen had been lacerated, exposing his large intestines.

Felix studied the opening. With care, but still worry for his friend, he crept through. His eyes traced over Tarzano and spotted the first aid kit still attached to his cargo pants.

"Alright," Felix said, digging his hands into Tarzano's medical bag, "let's get to work."

CHAPTER 75

Felix American Pony

"You're gonna be alright," Felix said to Tarzano as he worked the Israeli Army-style bandage.

Tarzano chortled. Blood and saliva leaked from his lips, "You sure about that?"

Felix gave a weak smile as he stared at the pink, serpentine tissue that was balled up on Tarzano's stomach.

"Sure," Felix grunted, "just like back at Artesia."

With glove-covered hands, Felix pushed the exposed organs further up. Taking the Israeli wrap, he wound it around the wound. Each time, Tarzano pulled his hands back so Felix could stretch the material across. Then, raking the hundred mile tape from Tarzano's kit, Felix cut six-inch stripes.

"100 mile-an hour tape?" Tarzano asked.

"Never go to the field without it," Felix replied as he placed the green strips across his stomach.

Tarzano groaned, "Now, how do we get out of here?"

"Gotham!" Felix yelled, as he looked through the crude opening. Gotham remained motionless on the ground. "Finally found a good use for those biceps and he's passed out!"

"I ain't outta the fight yet!" Gotham called out.

"I got Tarzano wrapped up," Felix said, "but he's hurting."

Through the detritus mist, Felix watched the Herculean-built man struggle to his feet. Gotham stumbled, falling back into the ground. Felix started to rush forward, but Gotham managed to get to his feet. Gotham, though waving left to right from fatigue, lifted his right hand up and beckoned them forward.

"Let's do this," he said.

With careful precision, the two men maneuvered Tarzano through the crude opening. Using Tarzano's rope, they hooked up a harness and wrapped it around Tarzano's shoulders. They then used the axe Felix had found and, using two half hitches, secured it by a square knot around its shaft. Felix climbed up and wrapped the rope over a piece of sturdy metal, forming a pulley.

Despite his fatigue, Gotham patted his biceps and replied, "Don't worry, I got you."

Felix nodded and, working with Tarzano, started to pull. Tarzano wrapped his legs around Felix's waist as they climbed, and Felix faced him similar to a jiu-jitsu position.

"No eye contact, Tarzano," Felix joked.

But Tarzano didn't laugh. Felix's gut tightened; he knew what that meant—Tarzano's injuries were too great. Felix started his climb up the makeshift wall. All his muscles stung as lactic acid rushed through his body.

"Argh!—" Gotham grunted as he pulled down, assisting in pulling them up. Felix continued to climb, Tarzano continued to clutch, and Gotham pulled with all his might. Because of the positioning, Gotham could only use his arms. From the corner of his eye, Felix could see Gotham straining. He gnashed his teeth as his face turned red and his throat swelled.

"We made it," Felix said, crawling onto the ground. He winced as burs penetrated his hands and knees. His lungs burned as he sucked in oxygen.

But despite all this, they had saved Tarzano.

"It was," Felix panted to himself, "it was worth it."

CHAPTER 76
Felix American Pony

While Felix and the others paused to catch their breaths, the monsters did not. The Titanoboa continued to constrict around the Gorgon as they battled. Dust clouds shot thirty feet into the air. Rocks and sediments shot out like projectiles.

The two monsters—locked in mortal combat—slammed against the side of the mountain. The physics of the fall shot them airborne. The Gorgon dug its paws into the snake. The serpent hit its head forward—digging its teeth into the Gorgon's shoulder.

WHAAM

The entangled melee slammed into the downed aircraft—barely missing the group of humans. The weight of the monsters collapsed in the center. They writhed in pain.

But while the impact fatigued their bodies, their pain only fueled the conflict's intensity. Their cries were loud and horrible, different than any other living beast.

Still fatigued and concussed, the Gorgon shot its massive snout forward and attempted to bite the serpent's belly. The scales shielded it and the snake re-constricted its horrible, slithering form around the Gorgon. It then shot its head forward into the Gorgon's ribs. Blood from both beasts flew through the air, covering the Chihuahuan Desert.

The Gorgon pulled its head back, looking for a new target. The Titanoboa saw this and, as the proto-mammalian pulled back, the snake rushed forward—stabbing its spear-shaped head into the Gorgon's throat.

Foamy discharge sprang from the Gorgon's mouth. It gagged. In a desperate effort, it swung its paws—claws extended. It cut against the Titanoboa's shield-like scales, penetrating. But the snake gave no release.

The Gorgon swung. Then, he swung again. Each time, the Gorgon made contact with the serpent's neck, just below its head. Each time, it exposed more and more of its internal muscles.

The Gorgon's eyes began to fog. Its visible weakness grew stronger. It swung—one more time.

WHAAM!

The Titanoboa yanked its head back, hissing and yowling in horrible and indescribable tones. A terrible slash ran downward from the top of its neck, exposing pink, soggy material.

Adrenaline rushed through the Gorgon's fading body. Overwhelming pain and exhaustion troubled the beast, but now, desperation had been replaced with hope.

The Gorgon was back in the fight.

CHAPTER 77

Jorge Mondragon

"Jorge," Brody said, pulling at the KS-23 that had been disassembled and tied down to Jorge's rucksack as they jumped back from the monster's collapse into the aircraft.

"What's going on?" Jorge yelled.

"Help me," Brody replied. "Help me fire this thing."

"The KS-23?" Jorge laughed. "The Russian 4-gauge shotgun?"

After Bill Bosworth was mauled to death by the black bear, it had been decided that a powerful weapon couldn't be abandoned.

"We have to finish them here," Brody yelled, finally freeing the weapon and working at its assembly.

"Aqui" Jorge waved the weapon, still conscious of the peril of their position. He took the gun, and, remembering the discussions with Bill, assembled, loaded, and charged the Russian shotgun.

"What's going on?" Gotham asked.

"We can't risk them surviving," Jorge said. "They gotta die."

"They'll do that themselves," Gotham panted and stood up. From his confusion and fatigue, he still clutched the emergency axe he had picked up in the chaos.

"I can't risk having them here," Jorge handed the shotgun to Brody.

Felix snorted and spat. He shook his head and smiled. "People," he said, adjusting his sling as they all fell away from the creatures. "You work in law enforcement and think you get to know people—but they'll always surprise you. Your job—the job you didn't want but…"

"Let us finish this!" Brody interrupted.

Jorge nodded, "Pl--"

But as he spoke, the monsters screamed at one another. In the melee, they rolled toward them. Brody raised the Russian shotgun. Jorge gripped Brody by the shoulder and forcefully pushed him laterally. Not to stop him, but to allow for a better angle.

BOOM!

BOOM!

The 4-gauge slugs slammed into the Titanoboa, causing pain so great it released the Gorgon. The Gorgon went in for the kill.

BANG BANG BANG

Fire from shotguns and pistols blasted into the beasts. Orange blasts exploded from the barrels.

Both monsters burst forward at the ground.

"No!" Gotham cried as the Titanoboa slithered over the supine, injured form of Tarzano—his gore smeared the ground underneath the snake as it slithered forward. Its horrible body smacked into Jorge, knocking him backward. He rolled, feet overhead, dust shooting up as he did.

"Tarzano!" Gotham screamed, axe in hand. Then, with ardent fervor, he swung. Gotham's axe penetrated the snake, sending massive gobs of blood outward with each hack.

BOOM!

The KS-23 sounded again. Smoke rose from the snake's body.

BOOM!

Undeterred, Gotham continued to hack.

Until finally, the head of the great snake fell free.

CHAPTER 78

Jorge Mondragon

"Get out of the way!" Jorge yelled at Gotham, who struggled to remain standing.

Still clutching the axe, the mercenary leader turned his head away from Jorge. Behind him, the Gorgon crept forward. The monster bared its fangs. Blood from its serpent foe dripped. Gore caked its feline-like whiskers. A hate-fueled flame filled the Gorgon's eyes.

"It's my turn," Jorge said. "I got this one."

Gotham stumbled out of the way. Jorge stepped forward. He felt hate rush through his body.

This monster had killed Enrique Esparza—bringing turmoil to the place he loved. The beast growled in a low, grave tone. Jorge could feel the subwoofer-like tones vibrate against his body.

"Here, kitty, kitty, kitty," Jorge whispered, charging the forend of his Keltec KSG.

The Gorgon shot forward, and Jorge released a shower of flame from his Underbarrel flamethrower. Amber flames jumped about on the Gorgon's face. It shut its eyes, shielding them.

But the beast's eyes weren't Jorge's intended target. Instead, he had blanketed the feline-like monster's whiskers in fire. The Gorgon's organic antennae were burnt to ash. Bits of gray smithereens littered the ground beneath it.

The Gorgon shook its head, fighting to turn away and run.

BANG BANG BANG

Jorge fired the Keltec KSG. Rounds beat against the Gorgon's throat and face.

With simultaneous efforts, both Felix and Brody fired.

Jorge's KSG ran empty. He dropped the shotgun and it fell to the ground. He drew his gold-colored Smith & Wesson XVR 460 Magnum.

He fired all six rounds. Firing with precise shots, all rounds hit the approaching beast.

"*Puedo* breathe; *puedo* fight!" Jorge said, and yanking the Kukri blade free from his vest, he sprinted forward.

CHAPTER 79

Jorge Mondragon

Jorge stabbed the Kukri blade underneath the Gorgon's throat. The Gorgon howled and Jorge's entire body erupted in goosebumps. He pushed his hand further, the Kukri blade sinking deeper into the monster's throat.

As the blade lacerated its tongue, the Gorgon stopped its cry. Now, it whimpered.

Jorge stopped. He felt his eyes water at the noise. His mind rushed to the cat—the one he had saved. He yanked the Kukri from the monster.

Slowly, he stepped back. The Gorgon continued its pitiful cry. Jorge felt the others look at him. Reverently, he studied the monster. For reasons unknown to Jorge, the beast stepped forward. It stumbled. It slammed into the earth. Its scaled face landed inches from Jorge's boot-covered toes. It twisted its neck—its head remaining on the Chihuahuan Desert floor. In its agony, it looked up at Jorge.

"I was supposed to protect life, buddy," Jorge stroked the side of the blade against the monster's snout.

Jorge didn't know the whole story. But he understood this: the monster was alone.

It killed—it harmed—it was guilty.

But while it was responsible, others had put it on this murderous path.

Jorge had been alone. Isolation had tormented them both. But Jorge had something this monster would never have— Jorge had family.

With the Kukri knife still in hand, Jorge looked around. He saw Brody, Tarzano, and Felix. He smiled as his mind rushed back to Mr. Gato.

Jorge had to kill this monster. He had to end its reign of terror. Yet, he pitied this creature. An abominable monster created by evil scientists and unleashed by anarchists.

To protect life, he had to kill.

But Jorge had grown tired of death.

"Take this cup from me," Jorge closed his eyes as he whispered.

As he opened them, he spotted Brody sprinting forward, bang stick in hand. He plunged it into the Gorgon's throat. Brody twisted the pole left and right, digging even further.

BOOM!

The monster's head exploded, covering all those around in gore.

CHAPTER 80

Jorge Mondragon

"Felix," Jorge sucked in air as his lungs heaved up and down.

"What's up?" Felix replied, his weapon still oriented on the Gorgon.

"I've got a job for you."

Felix turned around and looked at Jorge, "I think I'm going to take a little break."

"No," Jorge pointed to the dead Titanoboa, "you're not."

"What?"

"Tarzano," Jorge said, "he's alive."

Despite his fatigue, Gotham sprang to his feet and, with an ugly shambling gait, sprinted to his friend.

"The snake must have pushed him down into the sand," Jorge said. "Trust me, trucks get stuck out here all the time."

Jorge watched as Gotham grabbed the back of Tarzano's vest and freed him.

"I've got to get him out of here," Gotham said.

"You can," Felix walked to Gotham. "But not as fast as I can."

Gotham stood up, his facial expression showing confusion.

"I'll ride him back to Farmer Market Road," Felix walked toward his zorse behind them. He grabbed the hybrid creature's bridle and drew him to Tarzano. "I'll have connectivity. I'll call for help then."

Jorge stepped forward and put his hand on Felix's shoulder. "You rode all the way here. I can ride back."

Felix smiled, "I know your history. You're a great rider…"

"*Pero…*"

"I'm faster," Felix said, his voice calm. As he spoke, he helped Tarzano on the zorse.

"This is crazy," Brody said.

"But we ain't got no choice," Jorge watched Felix climb onto the zorse.

Then, he saw it. On Felix's naked back, toward the shoulder were the initials HNIRC and the word "Champion" tattooed in Minstrel-style font beneath.

Despite the severity of the situation, Jorge felt his stomach twist and his eyes bulge.

Horse Nations Indian Relay Council … Champion.

Growing up in West Texas, Jorge had been to rodeos. But an Indian relay was different. Competitors rode bare-back on their ink-decorated horses around the track in the intense Montana heat.

He's right, Jorge thought. *He's the right guy for this job.*

"Ride on, Felix!" Jorge nodded.

Felix said nothing as he dug his heels into the side of the zorse. A dust cloud rose skyward as the animal carried the two men south.

CHAPTER 81

Jorge Mondragon

Jorge watched as the zorse, with its riders, sprinted from El Solitario. From the volcano, they traveled south through Big Bend State Park.

"Well," Jorge sighed and looked around at the chaos, "looks like we're still walking."

"The danger isn't gone," Brody said as he wrapped his arm near the snake bite. "The monsters are dead, but the ecosystem is still changed."

Gotham propped himself up, leaning on the axe as he rested it on the Titanoboa's carcass. "This desert heat alone will kill ya," he croaked.

Jorge opened his mouth, about to say it was a dry heat. But a cell phone rang, silencing everyone.

"*¿Que es eso?*" Gotham asked.

Jorge scratched his head, caught off guard by the ringing sound.

"It's you," Brody pointed at Jorge.

Jorge's mouth gaped open. There was never a cell phone signal in this area.

How can I get a phone call?

He scanned his vest. His hand went into the compartment where he kept his phone.

"Unidentified Number" ran across the screen. Jorge held it out in front of him, showing the others.

"Answer it!" Gotham said.

Jorge flinched, then answered the call and brought the phone to his ear. He said nothing.

"Hay-lo, Mr. Mondragon," a man with a thick cockney accent spoke from the other side.

Jorge pulled the phone from his head and studied the screen. "Who is this?" Jorge asked as he put the phone back to his ear.

"Not so much *who* I am," the man said, "but who my *organization* is."

"The anarchists who shot down that plane?"

"I am a... representative of the person who owned the plane," the voice said.

"The Albuquerque Air Force? *La Frontera*...?"

"All you need to know is that we are an organization—like yours— who doesn't desire an armed conflict."

"I'd hardly call—"

"My employer wishes to thank you for recovering our aircraft—"

"What?"

"It appears US Government agencies have defeated the jammer system that thwarted our ability to recover our aircraft. As a courtesy, my employer wishes to convey the imminent scuttle of the vessel..."

"*Que?*"

"My organization recommends the urgent exodus from the immediate area..."

"What is a scuttle?" Jorge yelled. This time, he caught Gotham's eyes as he spoke.

"That's a naval term," Felix yelled, "to destroy your ship."

"But how can you destroy your plane," Jorge studied the damaged vessel, "when you're not here?"

"As stated previously," the voice said, "our systems have returned. Following our standard operating procedure, the vessel will be scuttled to mitigate the risk of incrimination..."

The man continued to speak. As he did, Jorge heard a short, single, automated-sounding tone, uncomfortably loud and high in pitch.

"Ah, scuttle," Jorge said, "now, I get it..."

Gotham ran to his position and grabbed his shoulders, "*Vamanos! Vamanos!*"

Brody looked side-to-side and started to run as well, "What's going on—"

"Run!" Jorge screamed, and the trio sprinted away from the downed aircraft.

Sandburs and other painful vegetation cut them as they ran. The lacerations only fueled them forward.

"*Abajo! Abajo!*" Gotham screamed.

"What?" Brody asked. Immediately, Jorge tackled him and pinned him to the ground.

BOOM!

Giant orange flames consumed the wreckage. Debris shot up and outward. Dust clouds composed of detritus hung in the sky.

"The plane!" Brody yelled.

That cartel plane had a destruction system, Jorge thought. *Controlled by its owners.*

A high-pitched squeal rang through Jorge's ears. He blinked and shook his head, trying to refocus.

"Look! Look!" Brody pointed into the sky. "It's a helicopter! That must be medivac, right?"

Jorge looked at Brody. He could see the confusion in the man's face and could tell the concussed man was trying to make sense of it.

"That helicopter," Brody nodded, "that's like an ambulance for us, right?"

A helicopter with a body identical to a US Army UH-60 but with a Santa Muerte figure painted on its nose flew above them. Jorge winced—how could he explain the situation to Brody in his current state?

He shook his head. "No, Brody... that chopper ain't friendly."

CHAPTER 82

Jorge Mondragon

Jorge watched as the La Frontera helicopter flew into the air. His body still stung from the blow. He felt a hand gripping his shoulder and saw Brody pointing to his vest.

"Phone call!" Brody screamed.

Jorge, embarrassed to have missed the ringing, shoved his hand in his vest and pulled the phone free. He put the device on speaker mode and answered.

"Hello?"

"Mr. Mondragon," the cockney-accented man spoke again. "Your friend has suffered serious injuries. Once the anarchists' jammer systems were destroyed, the surveillance technology from our downed aircraft returned. We were able to observe the entirety of Mr. Salvatore-Jones' peril. I assure you, Mr. Salvatore-Jones will be given the best medical care our organization can provide. Once healed, he shall be returned."

"Ugh," Jorge blinked, trying to understand the situation, *"...gracias?"*

The phone chimed in treble and bass pitches, frustrating Jorge, who couldn't determine if he had heard the tones or if his tinnitus confused him. Looking at the phone screen, he read the words "call ended."

"Huh?"

"What just happened?" Brody yelled.

"I don't really know," Jorge replied. *"Pero...* I think the cartel is trying to pick up the tab."

"What?" Brody yelled.

"I think we averted the second Mexican Border War," Jorge wiped sweat from his brow with a handkerchief.

"We mighta avoided that," Brody said, "but I wouldn't say we came out unscathed."

Jorge looked over the scene of chaos. The flames flickered from the downed cartel aircraft. Dust and vegetation hung in the air as the debris clouds had not yet dissipated. Portions of the great Titanoboa now melted as burning hunks had slammed into the carcass. An indescribable odor stung Jorge's nostrils, forcing him to use the lower part of his nose and mouth. The headless Gorgon decorated the soil like a horrific, organic statue. Its brain matter, bits of fangs, ocular tissues, and tongue caked the already chaotic scene with even more depravity.

So much death, Jorge thought, *so much terror.*

But despite all this evil that had threatened his home, they had stood and fought. Jorge looked over and saw his friend, Brody, still clutching the bang stick.

"No," Jorge said, "I'd say we all came out changed."

The End

Check out other great

Dinosaur Thrillers!

P.K. Hawkins

THE LOST ISLAND

Scientists Dr. Eccleston and Dr. Lerner have done many routine expeditions for the Skurzon Corporation in the past, helping the company search the ocean for newly available resources freed by melting ice. They're expecting to maybe find oil at the bottom of the Arctic Sea. What they aren't expecting is a lost island that defies all scientific understanding. When something comes out of the sea and destroys their research vessel, the scientists and the rest of the crew are forced into a game of survival against forces no human being has ever seen alive. If they can survive the giant insect swarms, the man-eating plants, and the dinosaurs, they might be able to live to tell the tale. But when each passing moment reveals murderers in their midst, their survival starts to look less and less likely.

William Meikle

THE LAND BELOW

A treasure hunt into the deepest cave system in Europe takes a turn for the worst. Now rather than treasure it is survival that is at the forefront of the spelunkers' thoughts. But their attempt to escape out of the dark deep places is thwarted. Men are not at home in the depths. But there are things that are, pale terrifying things. Huge things. Things red in tooth and claw.

Check out other great

Dinosaur Thrillers!

Julian Michael Carver

TRIASSIC

After spending many years in artificial hypersleep, a handful of survivors of the exploration vessel Supernova awaken to find their ship torn to shreds. They are unsure of what happened in space or how they crashed into an uncharted planet. Upon exploration of the new world, they soon realize their destination: The Triassic, the first chapter of the Mesozoic Era. A plan is formulated to escape this terrifying landscape plagued with dinosaurs and prehistoric beasts. The survivors soon discover that there may be an even larger threat looming under the trees than just the dinosaurs, threatening to cut their mission short and trap them all forever in the primitive depths of the Triassic.

Hugo Navikov

THE FOUND WORLD

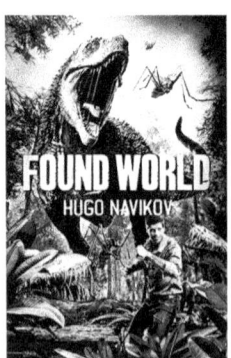

A powerful global cabal wants adventurer Brett Russell to retrieve a superweapon stolen by the scientist who built it. To entice him to travel underneath one of the most dangerous volcanoes on Earth to find the scientist, this shadowy organization will pay him the only thing he cares about: information that will allow him to avenge his family's murder. But before he can get paid, he and his team must enter an underground hellscape of killer plants, giant insects, terrifying dinosaurs, and an army of other predators never previously seen by man. At the end of this journey awaits a revelation that could alter the fate of mankind ... if they can make it back from this horrifying found world.

Check out other great
Dinosaur Thrillers!

Rick Poldark
PRIMORDIAL ISLAND

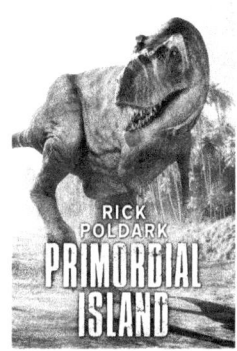

During a violent storm Flight 207 crash-lands in the South China Sea. Poseidon Tech tracks the wreckage to an uncharted island and dispatches a curious salvage team—two paleontologists, a biologist specializing in animal behavior, a botanist, and a nefarious big game hunter. Escorted by a heavily-armed security team, they cut through the jungle and quickly find themselves in a terrifying fight for survival, running a deadly gauntlet of prehistoric predators. In their quest for the flight recorder, they uncover the mystery of the island's existence and discover an arcane force that will tip the balance of power on the primordial island. Things are not as they seem as they race against time to survive the island's man-eating dinosaurs and make it back home in one piece.

P.K. Hawkins
SUBTERRANEA

Fall, 1985. The small town of Kettle Hollow barely shows up on any maps, and four young friends are used to taking their BMX's outside of town in an effort to find anything interesting to do. But tonight their tendency to go off by themselves may have saved them, and also forced them into the adventure of a lifetime.While they were away, Kettle Hollow has been locked down by the government, and a portal to another world has opened on Main Street. It's a world deep below the ground, a world where dinosaurs roam free, where giant plants and mutant insects hunt for prey. It's also a world where all their family and friends have been kidnapped for sinister purposes. Now, with time running out before the portal closes, the four friends must brave the unknown to save their loved ones. Time is running out, and in the darkened tunnels of Subterranea, something is hunting them.

www.ingramcontent.com/pod-product-compliance
Lightning Source LLC
Chambersburg PA
CBHW061235170626
46809CB00007B/2685